Later that night, Casey went to the top of the stairs. The lightning flashed and the wind moaned like a lonely ghost. In the dark shadows, the living room sofa looked like a beast ready to pounce.

Casey shivered in her thin nightgown. Her slender arms were covered with goose bumps. She didn't want to go downstairs. She didn't dare. But her Slime Monster was missing and she had to find him.

Casey crept barefoot down the carpeted steps. Suddenly a brilliant flash lit the stairwell and a crack of thunder ripped open the night. In that instant, Casey saw her Slime Monster sitting on the windowsill, grinning down at her. Casey gasped. Her heart was bouncing around inside her chest like a paddleball and her throat was so tight she could hardly breathe.

Another lightning flash lit up the windowsill. The Slime Monster was gone!

Join the Team!

Do you watch GHOSTWRITER on PBS? Then you know that when you read and write to solve a mystery or unravel a puzzle, you're using the same smarts and skills the Ghostwriter Team uses.

We hope you'll join the team and read along to help solve the mysterious and puzzling goings-on in all of the GHOSTWRITER books!

Attack of the Slime Monster

by Carin Greenberg Baker

A Children's Television Workshop Book

Bantam Books
New York Toronto London
Sydney Auckland

ghostwriter®

ATTACK OF THE SLIME MONSTER

A Bantam Book / May 1996

 ® *is a registered trademark of Children's Television Workshop.*
Ghostwriter™ and ● *are*
trademarks of Children's Television Workshop.
All rights reserved. Used under authorization.

Written by Carin Greenberg Baker
Cover design by Marietta Anastassatos

ISBN 0-553-48393-5

Published simultaneously in the United States and Canada

Bantam Books are published by Bantam Books, a division of
Bantam Doubleday Dell Publishing Group, Inc. Its trademark,
consisting of the words "Bantam Books" and the portrayal of a
rooster, is Registered in U.S. Patent and Trademark Office and
in other countries. Marca Registrada. Bantam Books, 1540
Broadway, New York, New York 10036.

PRINTED IN THE UNITED STATES OF AMERICA

OPM   0 9 8 7 6 5 4 3 2 1

Chapter One

"Sure you can borrow my boom box, Tina," said Lenni Frazier. "What's a party without tunes?"

Lenni paced the wooden floor of the loft she shared with her father, talking into the cordless phone wedged between her chin and her shoulder. It seemed like the perfect day. Late-afternoon sunlight streamed through the gated windows. School had just let out for the summer. Twelve-year-old Lenni planned to spend her time going to the beach, making music, and hanging out with her best friends, the Ghostwriter Team. Best of all, her friend Tina Nguyen was throwing an end-of-school party on Sunday, and the whole team was invited.

It *seemed* like the perfect day.

"I want some really hot dance tunes," Tina was saying on the other end of the line. "How 'bout that new CD from Boyz Will Be Boyz?"

Whenever anyone on the team had a question

about music, they always asked Lenni. Her father was a jazz musician, and Lenni had been singing and writing songs almost since she could talk.

" 'Love Groove?' " Lenni fast-forwarded through the song tracks in her mind. "Nah," she said. "Too mellow."

"I like the Boyz!" piped up a voice from the other end of the loft. Eight-year-old Casey Austin sat hunched over the kitchen counter, writing in a notebook. Her black curly hair hung down the back of her blue denim jumper.

Lenni couldn't see what Casey was writing, but an eerie greenish glow hovered over the notebook. If Lenni hadn't seen the glow before, she might have been scared. She might have thought aliens were invading from another planet. But the glow wasn't aliens. It was Ghostwriter.

Ghostwriter was a real ghost, although he didn't remember who he'd been when he was alive. Only the kids on the Ghostwriter Team could communicate with him. Ghostwriter had contacted Lenni's friend, Jamal Jenkins, by writing to Jamal on his computer. Jamal had thought he was going crazy, because his grandmother and his sister couldn't see Ghostwriter. But then Lenni was able to see Ghostwriter, too. The other kids who could see Ghostwriter were Alex and Gaby Fernandez, who lived behind their family's store downstairs from Lenni's loft; Hector Carrero; Tina; and Casey, who was Jamal's cousin.

Ghostwriter communicated by writing to Lenni and her friends. He couldn't see them, but he could feel what they were feeling and he could read any words anywhere. After Ghostwriter had helped Lenni and her friends solve their first mystery, they had given themselves their official name: the Ghostwriter Team.

"What about Nana Strawberry?" Lenni suggested as she paced the wooden floor. "She's got that song, 'Bouncing Baby Girl.'" She bopped as she sang, "'I'm your baby, baby. Come on and dance with me. . . .'"

As she sang in her low, clear voice, she was unaware of the presence behind her.

"'Pick me up, give me love, bounce me on your knee. . . .'"

The presence had feet. Feet that were inching slowly toward Lenni as it prepared to pounce.

"'Spin me till I'm dizzy, let's go for a twirl. I'm your baby, baby. I'm your bouncing baby—' Aaaaaaaaaaagh!" Lenni screamed as a hideous purple creature leaped up behind her shoulder. Red-veined eyes popped out of its head and purple goo oozed out of its twisted mouth. It wore a shiny black raincoat and heavy workboots and had large purple hands.

"Gotcha!" Casey shouted, jumping out from behind Lenni. She held the purple creature in her hands and laughed hysterically.

Lenni didn't see what was so funny. Her heart was

bouncing around inside her chest like a paddleball and her throat was so tight she could hardly breathe. "What *is* that thing?" she demanded, backing away from Casey.

"It's Gooey Gus, the Slime Monster," Casey answered proudly. "Isn't he gross?" Casey pushed a button on top of the monster's head. Purple goo shot straight out of the monster's mouth and into Casey's.

Lenni had never seen anything so disgusting in her entire life.

"Lenni? Lenni? Are you okay?" Tina asked over the phone. Lenni had almost forgotten Tina was still on the line.

"Uh, yeah," Lenni said distractedly. "Look, why don't you just come over and we'll go over my CDs together, okay?"

"Sure," Tina said, and hung up.

Lenni looked back at Casey, who was happily chewing on a giant wad of something. "What is that stuff?" Lenni asked.

"Grape bubble gum!" Casey stuck her purple-covered tongue out of her mouth, and a shiny purple bubble expanded slowly until it was almost the size of her face.

"Looks more like slime," Lenni observed.

The bubble popped. "That's 'cause he's the Slime Monster!" Casey said.

"What is he? Some kind of doll?"

"He's not a doll. He's an *action figure*," Casey explained. "And there's a great story about where he came from. See, it all started at this bubble-gum factory. One day, the guy who was supposed to be mixing up the bubble gum fell asleep at the controls. The bubble gum got too hot, then too much sugar got poured in. There was a big explosion, and . . . *Boom!* Gooey Gus, the Slime Monster, was born!"

Casey crouched down on the floor with the action figure and slowly raised him above her head as she continued her tale. "He rose up out of the bubble gum all slimy and twisted and gross-looking. He was one mean chunk of chewing gum." Casey pressed another button in the Slime Monster's back.

"I'm *burning* mad! I'm *steaming* mad!" the monster said in a gritty, growly voice.

Lenni laughed. This little guy was starting to grow on her. In fact, he was almost kind of cute. Casey pressed the button in his back again.

"You laughing at me? You laughing at *me?*" the monster snarled.

"Touchy, isn't he?" Lenni asked.

"He's very sensitive. The Slime Monster doesn't like it when people make fun of him. And when he gets mad . . ." Casey pressed the button one more time.

"Slime, anyone?" the monster asked.

Casey pressed another button on top of the action figure's head. More purple slime shot out of his mouth. Lenni opened her mouth to catch it. The bubble gum was soft and sweet and tasted like grape juice.

"Yum!" Lenni said.

A streak of green light flew off Casey's notebook and burrowed under the Slime Monster's raincoat. It was Ghostwriter.

"What's he doing?" Lenni wondered.

Casey turned the action figure over and lifted up the raincoat. Ghostwriter was glowing on words printed on the monster's back: WARNING: DO NOT OVERHEAT!

"Oh yeah," Casey said. "They put that on all the slime monsters."

"But why?" Lenni asked. "Who would overheat a doll? It's not like you're going to stick him in the microwave or anything."

"You never know," Casey said. "Some kids might leave him out in the sun too long on a really hot day and the Slime Monster could explode or something! Then there'd be slime all over the place. It would be dripping off the walls and oozing over the ground—hey! That sounds pretty scary, doesn't it? Maybe I'll put that in my story." Casey ran back to the kitchen counter and hopped up on a stool. She pulled the notebook toward her and grabbed her pencil.

Lenni followed Casey and tried to read the notebook over Casey's shoulder. "What story?" she asked.

"The one I'm writing for the Slime Monster contest," Casey answered. "Whoever writes the scariest, creepiest story wins. But the rules say 'no blood and no guns.' Like, you can't blow anybody's head off."

"I'm glad to hear that." Lenni hated all the violence on TV and in the movies.

"Yeah," Casey agreed, "but it's a lot harder to make it scary, and I don't have much time. The deadline's Monday!"

"Can I see what you've written?" Lenni asked.

Casey slid the notebook across the counter toward Lenni. Ghostwriter hopped onto the notebook and read along with Lenni:

Attack of the Slime Monster
by Casey Austin

Once there was a girl named Casey who wanted Gooey Gus, the Slime Monster. She thought it would be fun to play with. But she was wrong. <u>Dead</u> wrong.

It all started about a week before Casey's birthday (which is July 2nd in case anyone reading this wants to buy me a present). Casey had seen the Slime Monster commercials on TV, so she started bugging her Grandma CeCe to get her one. Grandma CeCe promised she'd look for a Slime Monster, but so far she hadn't been able to find one. The monster was just too popular and all the toy stores were sold out.

Casey was beginning to lose hope. It looked like she'd never get a Slime Monster. Then, one day when Casey and Grandma were in the living room, her cousin Jamal came through the front door carrying a big box covered with wrapping paper. Casey started jumping up and down. She knew what was in that box. It was a Slime Monster. It just had to be!

"Happy birthday, little cuz," Jamal said, putting the box in Casey's lap.

Casey ripped the paper off the box. On the side of the package was a picture of a globby purple face with bulgy eyes.

"Gooey Gus, the Slime Monster!" Casey cried happily. "You found one!" She started to open the box, but Jamal stopped her.

"Just a second, Casey," he said. "You'd better be careful opening that box. It was a long walk home from the toy store, and it's really hot outside. You know what they say about the Slime Monster."

"No, what do they say?" Grandma asked.

Casey knew. " 'Warning: Do not overheat,' " she told her grandmother.

Grandma looked worried. "I don't like the sound of that."

Casey looked over at Jamal. He was covering his mouth with his hand, but she could tell he was smiling. Jamal was up to something, but he should have known better than to try to fool her. When it came to jokes and tricks, nobody was better than Casey.

"Don't worry about it," Casey told her grand-mother as she opened the Slime Monster box. "Jamal's just trying to scare—Aaaaaaaaaah! Snakes!" Casey screamed and backed away from the box. Grandma CeCe jumped, too.

The box was filled with quivering, scaly snakes, curled all over each other and piled on top of each other. Casey was afraid one of them would jump out and bite her. Then she realized the snakes were quivering because <u>she</u> was quivering. They weren't real. They just looked real.

"Gotcha!" laughed Jamal. "I've been waiting to get you back ever since you hid those snakes in my drawer last year!"

Casey was a good sport. It's not like she couldn't take a joke. But the snakes she'd put in Jamal's drawer were made of paper. They weren't scary and real-looking like these. Jamal's trick was just plain mean.

Casey reached through the fake rubber snakes and pulled the Slime Monster action figure out of the box. Then she lunged at Jamal with it. "I'll get you!" Casey shouted, chasing him around the living room.

Jamal jumped over the coffee table and ran around behind the couch. "You gotta catch me first!" He laughed.

Jamal may have been five years older than Casey, but that didn't mean he was faster or smarter. Casey ran after her cousin and squirted him with Slime Monster slime. Unfortunately, Jamal ducked just in time. The slime didn't hit him. It hit Grandma CeCe.

Casey smiled nervously, hoping Grandma would think this was a funny joke. But Grandma didn't seem to be in a joking mood.

Grandma CeCe held out her hand. "Okay, young lady," she said sternly. "Hand it over."

Glumly, Casey gave Gooey Gus to Grandma.

"Gotcha again!" Jamal laughed.

It was bad enough that Jamal had tricked Casey. But now he'd made her lose the toy she'd been waiting so long for. And he looked so <u>happy</u> about it!

Casey was mad. Burning mad. She glared at her cousin. "You laughing at me?" she snarled. She swore she'd get her revenge.

Chapter Two

L enni looked up from Casey's notebook. "This is a really great story!" she said. "So what happened? *Did* Casey get her revenge?"

"Keep reading," Casey told her.

Lenni turned the page.

"Maybe I shouldn't have gotten so mad at Jamal," Casey said to her Slime Monster the next day. She sat on the couch in the living room holding the action figure. "Jamal was just trying to be funny. And maybe I deserved it after all the tricks I played on him. What do you think, Slimy?"

The Slime Monster opened its mouth and its head turned to look at Casey. "I'm <u>burning</u> mad!" he answered. "I'm <u>steaming</u> mad!"

Casey screamed so loud the windows shook and the doors rattled. She threw the monster down on the couch. "Jamal! Jamal!" she cried. "Come quick!"

Jamal ran into the room from the kitchen. "What's the matter?"

Casey didn't go near the couch. She just pointed at the slimy purple creature that stared up at the ceiling with bloodshot eyes. "It . . . talked . . ." she whispered. "Could it be . . . alive?"

Jamal burst out laughing. "Sorry, Casey," he said. You almost got me, but I don't fool that easily. All Slime Monsters talk."

"But this Slime Monster doesn't have any batteries!" she squeaked.

Jamal looked confused. "What are you talking about?"

Casey reached into the Slime Monster box and pulled out a pair of C batteries. They were still covered in clear plastic. "See?" Casey said. "I never unwrapped them."

Jamal smiled. "You don't give up!" He strolled over to the couch and picked up the action figure. "Lemme guess. You put in another pair of batteries, right?" Lifting up the Slime Monster's raincoat, Jamal stuck his thumbnail under the battery compartment lid. When he popped it open and looked inside, the smile slid off his face. The battery compartment was empty!

Jamal turned the Slime Monster over and looked at its face. It seemed to be staring back at Jamal. "Slime, anyone?" the Slime Monster asked.

"Aaaaagh!" Jamal dropped the monster and hid behind the couch.

Casey had been trying not to laugh, but now she let go. Her plan had worked perfectly! She reached behind a pillow on the couch and pulled out a mini-tape recorder, which was still running. "You laughing at me?" asked the Slime Monster's taped voice. "You laughing at me?"

"Gotcha!" Casey said to Jamal.

Jamal looked embarrassed. "You sure did." He picked up the Slime Monster from the floor and stared into its red-veined eyes. "For a minute there, I really thought . . ." His voice trailed off. He looked at Casey. "So?" he asked. "Are we even now? Truce?"

"Truce," Casey said as she shook Jamal's hand.

"Well?" Casey asked as Lenni closed the notebook. "What do you think of my story so far?"

Lenni pushed her straight brown hair behind one ear. "It's funny," she said. "It's full of jokes and tricks, just like you."

This was what Casey had been afraid of. She'd had a feeling, as she was writing, that her story wasn't very scary. Lenni had just confirmed it.

Casey sighed. "I'm never going to win this contest. I want it to be so scary that anyone who reads it won't be able to sleep at night! I want people's *hair* to stand on end."

"You want their blood to run cold?" Lenni asked.

Casey nodded. "Exactly. But I guess it's just not going to happen."

Lenni's brown eyes grew thoughtful. "Maybe I could help you make it scarier," she offered. "Or would that be cheating?"

"No!" Casey said quickly. "The rules said kids can work together. You want to?"

"Sure! I like contests." Lenni picked up Casey's notebook and walked over to her computer on a table near the couch. "You mind if I type it? It will go faster."

Casey liked the sound of that. The deadline was getting closer and closer. "Fast is good," Casey said.

Lenni sat down and turned on the computer. "Scary and creepy . . ." she murmured, staring at the blank screen.

"But no blood and no guns," Casey reminded her.

"Right." Lenni started to type:

Later that day, Casey came downstairs.

Lenni frowned. "This isn't scary enough."

There was a flash of light, then more words appeared on the computer screen. It was Ghostwriter sending them a message:

What are you doing?

Lenni quickly typed her answer:

"We're trying to make Casey's story scarier."

Why don't you set the story at night? Ghostwriter suggested.

"Yeah," Casey agreed. "Nighttime's much scarier than daytime."

Lenni deleted *day* and, in its place, typed *night*. Lenni's forehead wrinkled. "This is better," she said. "But it could still be scarier. We need more atmosphere."

"More what?" Casey asked.

"We need to choose words to describe the setting so it *feels* scary. Like, we should add thunder and lightning and stuff."

"Or wolves," Casey suggested. "They're scary."

"But who would believe it?" Lenni asked. "There aren't any wolves in Brooklyn."

"Oh yeah," Casey said.

Lenni began to type again:

The lightning flashed and the wind

"Whistled?" Lenni asked.

"No," Casey said. "Sounds too cheerful. How 'bout whispered?"

"Shivered?"

"Groaned?"

"Moaned?" Lenni tried.

Casey liked that one. "Yeah," she said. " 'The wind moaned.' That sounds creepy."

Lenni typed:

The lightning flashed and the wind moaned

Ghostwriter's glow filled the computer screen again as he added to what Lenni had written:

The lightning flashed and the wind moaned like a lonely ghost.

"Now *that's* what I call atmosphere," Lenni said approvingly.

Casey shivered as she read the words on the computer screen. This story was getting so scary she was afraid *she* wouldn't be able to sleep at night. Lenni's fingers clicked over the keyboard as she adjusted and picked up the story:

Later that night, Casey went to the top of the stairs. The lightning flashed and the wind moaned like a lonely ghost. In the dark shadows, the living room sofa looked like a beast ready to pounce.

Casey shivered in her thin nightgown. Her slender arms were covered with goose bumps. She didn't want to go downstairs. She didn't dare. But her Slime Monster was missing and she had to find him.

Casey crept barefoot down the carpeted steps. Suddenly, a brilliant flash lit the stairwell, and a crack of thunder ripped open the night. In that instant, Casey saw her Slime Monster sitting on the windowsill, grinning down at her. Casey gasped. Her heart was pounding like a sledgehammer.

There's nothing to be afraid of, she tried to tell herself. *He's just a harmless little—*

Another lightning flash lit up the windowsill. The Slime Monster was gone! Then came thunder so overpowering it vibrated in her bones. Casey clutched the banister. Where could the Slime Monster have gone? It couldn't just get up and walk away. To do that, he would have to be alive, and there was no way . . .

Thump! Thump! Thump! came a soft, persistent knock on the door.

Casey's eyes grew as big as tennis balls. Who— or what—would come out on a night like this?

There's only one way to find out, Casey told herself. Bravely, she let go of the banister and, with shaking legs, crept to the bottom of the stairs.

Thump! Thump! Thump!

"Who is it?" Casey whispered as she approached the door.

"I'm *burning* mad!" came a voice from the other side. "I'm *steaming* mad!"

Casey gave a nervous laugh. She'd just figured the whole thing out. It was Jamal on the other side of the door. He'd taken her tape recorder and was trying to play the same trick on her that she'd played on him.

"I know it's you," Casey tried to shout, but her voice came out strangled.

The doorknob rattled.

"Jamal?" Casey called.

17

There was no answer. Maybe Jamal was still so mad at Casey for her last trick that he wasn't talking to her.

"Okay," Casey said. "I'm sorry for all the jokes I ever pulled on you, but it's over now. We called a truce, remember?"

The doorknob began to turn. Casey was starting to think that whoever was behind the door wasn't Jamal. Casey slowly backed away from the door. Suddenly, from behind her, a slimy purple hand clamped down on her shoulder. She screamed.

"Aaaaaaaaaaaaaah!"

Chapter Three

As Lenni continued typing the story, a hand clamped down on her shoulder. She screamed.

"*Aaaaaaaaaaaah!*"

Lenni whipped around and found herself staring into the handsome face of Alex Fernandez. Thirteen-year-old Alex was tall and lean and had close-cropped black hair. His almond-shaped eyes were brown and he had a strong chin. Lots of girls thought Alex was a total hunk, but Lenni had known him so long it was hard to see him as anything but a friend.

"Sorry I scared you," Alex said. "Casey let us in."

"He has that effect on all the girls," teased Alex's nine-year-old sister, Gaby, who was behind him. Like Alex, she was tall and thin, but it was hard to see how skinny she was under her oversized sweatshirt and baggy shorts. Her dark, curly hair was pulled up in a high ponytail, and she wore big gold hoop earrings.

"What are you writing?" Alex asked Lenni, looking over her shoulder at the computer.

Gaby had already read what was on the screen. "This must be for the Slime Monster contest!" she exclaimed. "Some kids in my class are entering."

"Oh no!" Casey joined the group at the computer. "More competition."

Gaby and Alex read the story in Casey's notebook and on the computer.

"Not bad," Gaby said when they were done.

"Did you think it was scary?" Casey asked hopefully.

Gaby shrugged. "I've read scarier. Like 'The Telltale Heart' by Edgar Allan Poe. Did you ever read that?"

Lenni and Casey shook their heads.

Gaby spoke in a hushed voice. "See, there's this guy. He murders an old man and buries him under the floor. Then the guy thinks he hears the old man's heart beating, louder, *louder, louder!* . . . until it drives the killer crazy."

Casey was impressed. "That *does* sound scary."

"I love being scared," Gaby said proudly.

"That's why she spends so much time looking in the mirror," Alex teased.

Casey's face brightened. "Hey, Gaby! You want to write some of our story? Maybe you could help make it scarier."

"Sure," Gaby said. Lenni got up and Gaby plunked down in front of the computer. She stared at the screen. "I think," she said slowly, "that we need to build more *suspense.*"

"What's that?" Casey asked.

"It's where you want to know what's going to happen next," Alex explained.

"Where you're *dying* to know what's going to happen next, even though you're scared to find out," Gaby added.

"Yeah. Definitely put some suspense in," Casey agreed.

"The question," said Gaby, placing her fingers on the keyboard, "is *how.*" She screwed up her mouth and wrinkled her nose. Then she closed her eyes tight.

"What are you doing?" Lenni asked.

"I'm thinking," Gaby said. Then her eyes popped open. "I've got it!" She started to type:

Suddenly, from behind her, a slimy purple hand clamped down on her shoulder. She screamed.

"Aaaaaaaaaaaaaah!"

Casey turned around and saw . . .

Jamal holding the Slime Monster. Jamal had put the doll's hand on Casey's shoulder to trick her. "Gotcha!" he said with a laugh.

Casey was mad at Jamal for tricking her again, but she was so happy he wasn't a *real* monster that she forgave him. "Ha ha," Casey said, taking the Slime Monster. She hugged him tight. The nightmare was over. Now she could go to bed.

There was a dry, rattling sound, like a dead man's bones rubbing against each other.

"What's that?" Jamal asked, staring at the front door.

The rattling grew louder, louder, **louder!**

Casey turned to see where Jamal was looking. The doorknob was rattling and jiggling like it was having its own private earthquake. Jamal started backing away from the door, a look of terror on his face.

Casey was trying not to get scared, but she had one question. If Jamal was here in the living room with her, then who was on the other side of the door? Squealing like a demon cat, the door slowly opened.

"Oh no!" Jamal whimpered. "Oh no!"

Casey was too scared even to look. She buried her face in Jamal's shirt. But she felt Jamal's fingers prying her face away from the fabric, forcing her to look at . . .

Alex Fernandez, bursting into the front hall. He was holding Casey's mini–tape recorder and grinning like a circus clown. "Gotcha twice!" he and Jamal shouted together. Jamal held up one of his hands and Alex slapped it. Then they both cracked up laughing.

"That was a great idea, Alex," Jamal said. "Thanks for helping me."

"Any time, bro," Alex said, handing the tape recorder back to Jamal.

Casey snatched the tape recorder, *her* tape recorder, away from Jamal. How could he do this to her? They'd called a truce, and he'd broken it. Boys had no honor. Alex must have put him up to it. Alex was always doing stuff like that. Like, the time he and Gaby and their parents went to Tung Hoy, the Chinese restaurant. When Gaby wasn't looking, Alex dumped all this stuff in her tea, like soy sauce and duck sauce and even those chopped-up little vegetable bits they put inside egg rolls . . .

". . . Earth to Gaby!" Alex was shouting, his hands cupped around his mouth like a megaphone. "Hul-*lo!* Anybody home?"

The waiters and chopsticks and round tables covered with white tablecloths faded away in Gaby's mind, and she found herself staring at the words on the computer monitor.

"What's all this stuff about egg rolls?" Lenni asked. "Does the Slime Monster like Chinese food?"

The Slime Monster! Gaby had gotten so caught up in remembering what a pain Alex was that she'd forgotten all about the monster. The story about the Chinese restaurant was good, though. Gaby made a mental note to remember it when she wrote her autobiography.

"Sorry," Gaby said. "I sort of got off track." She deleted the section about the restaurant.

"Now what?" Alex asked.

"Put in more suspense!" Casey pleaded. "And atmosphere. We've got to win this contest."

Atmosphere. Gaby thought about the scary places she wanted to send her brother. "How 'bout we put Alex and Jamal in a haunted house with cobwebs and spiders?"

"Or what if the Slime Monster had this hangout where he keeps his victims?" Alex suggested. "It could be all cold and wet and smelly—"

"How 'bout we send them down a dark, deserted alley?" Casey asked. "Characters in scary stories are always taking stupid shortcuts."

"Yeah!" Gaby agreed. Casey's suggestion had given her a great idea. She started to type again.

The next day, on their way home from school, Jamal and Alex took a shortcut through a dark and deserted alley. They weren't paying attention to where they were going because they were too busy talking about the joke they had pulled on Casey. Too bad they were so full of themselves. Too bad they made that turn. But it was too late now . . .

"That was some joke we pulled on Casey," Jamal said with a smirk.

"You don't think she's gonna try to get us back, do you?" Alex worried. Alex liked to talk big about how brave he was, but he was really just a scaredy-cat inside.

"Nah," Jamal said. "I think Casey's too scared to play this game anymore, and that's fine with me."

Squish, squish, squish, squish.

Alex stopped short. "What was that?"

"What was what?" Jamal asked.

Alex stood absolutely still and listened for something. There was dead silence. Alex shrugged and kept on walking. "I guess it wasn't anything."

Squish, squish, squish, squish.

There it was again! It sounded to Alex like there was somebody following them, but he'd never heard footsteps like these before. Quick and soft and sloppy like someone hurrying through mud.

Alex looked back over his shoulder. All he saw was a narrow alleyway with cracked pavement and dented garbage cans. Above him, fire escapes zigzagged up the brick walls to a narrow band of sky.

"What?" Jamal demanded.

Alex laughed nervously. "I guess this Gotcha game's starting to get to me. I thought I heard footsteps."

The boys kept on walking.

"Look, Alex," Jamal said. "Even if the game's not over, what's the worst thing Casey could do? Put a whoopee cushion on my desk chair? Or put a fake spider on the counter when you're working at the bodega?" The bodega was the store Alex's parents owned.

Alex had to laugh at himself. "You're right," he agreed. "I shouldn't let my imagination—"

Squish, squish, squish, squish.

Alex wheeled around so fast his sneakers squeaked against the pavement. And when he looked down, he almost died of fright.

"Jamal!" he cried, grabbing his friend's arm and pointing.

A few feet away, grinning up at them with an evil red stare, stood the Slime Monster.

Alex was ready to run, but Jamal wouldn't let him. "Don't you get it? It's another Gotcha!" Jamal cupped his hands and shouted. "Very funny, Casey!"

There was no answer.

Alex couldn't let Jamal see how afraid he was. He had to pretend to be brave. "Yeah, Gaby!" he yelled. "I bet you're in on this, too, right?"

There was the eerie, echoey sound of children laughing, but it could have been anybody's children.

"Come on out, Casey," Jamal said, putting on that grown-up voice he had even though he was only thirteen years old. "Where are you hiding?" He took the lid of a garbage can and looked inside.

Alex looked behind another garbage can. Maybe Casey or Gaby really was hiding nearby.

But after searching the alley for several minutes, there was no sign of either of them.

"Okay," Jamal said finally. "So they got away real fast. That was a good Gotcha."

"Are you *sure* it was a Gotcha?" Alex asked Jamal.

"Of course it was," Jamal replied with irritation. "What else could it be?"

The Slime Monster stared up at them with a snaggle-toothed grin. He seemed to be laughing at them. Or was it just Alex's imagination? But Alex hadn't imagined those soft, squishy footsteps. Was it possible the Slime Monster had followed them all by himself?

"I'm going home to talk to Gaby," Alex said. "*She'll* have the answer."

Chapter Four

Alex pushed open the glass door of the bodega and looked around for Gaby. She wasn't sweeping the narrow aisles between the shelves of food. She wasn't at the refrigerator case by the wall, loading in containers of milk or soda. She wasn't at the freezer, either, sneaking an ice-cream sandwich like she did sometimes when she thought no one was looking. The only person in the bodega was Alex's father. He stood behind the counter at the cash register, talking on the phone.

"Papa!" Alex said, signaling to his father that he needed to speak to him. But Eduardo Fernandez would not be disturbed. He was arguing with somebody about the price of fixing his truck. Alex's parents had bought a used truck last year and it was always breaking down. Alex's father seemed pretty angry. Alex knew better than to interrupt him when he was in a mood like this.

Alex headed for the double door at the back of the bodega that led to the Fernandezes' apartment, but a delicious smell stopped him. It was rich and warm and made his mouth water.

There was a table set up at the end of the counter. On the table was a tall, stainless steel Crock-Pot, and in front of the pot was a sign: AR- ROZ CON POLLO—NICE AND HOT! $2.50 A BOWL. Chicken with rice! That was one of Alex's favorite dishes. Alex stopped by the Crock-Pot and lifted the lid. Inside, chunks of tender chicken rested on a bed of yellow rice.

Alex breathed in deeply through his nose. Mmm! Maybe he'd stop and have a bite. Then he remembered he was on Gaby's trail. There was no time. Alex marched down the hallway to Gaby's room. He paused outside Gaby's door, listening to see if his sister would say anything about the prank she'd just pulled in the alley. He heard Casey's voice first.

"What's a five-letter word beginning with s that means 'hot water vapor?'" she asked.

Alex edged around the door frame and peeked into the room. Casey was sitting on Gaby's bed in a corner of the room, looking at a crossword puzzle book. Gaby sat at her desk, braiding strings of red licorice.

"Steam," Gaby said, taking a bite of her licorice braid.

So that's what they were up to! They were pretending they'd been in Gaby's room all along to make it look like they'd never been in the alley. Well, Alex wasn't falling for it. He stormed into the room.

"Hey!" Gaby complained. "Don't you knock?"

Alex ignored Gaby. "You two must think you're pretty funny."

The girls looked at him like he was crazy (not the first time this had ever happened to him). "What are you talking about?" Casey asked.

"That little joke you pulled," Alex said accusingly. "Don't play dumb. I know you two were following us with that Slime Monster. How'd you get away so fast?"

Gaby looked genuinely confused. "Alex, I swear we didn't do anything."

"Did you say you've seen my Slime Monster?" Casey asked. "I've been searching all over for him since last night. He just disappeared."

The girls looked as if they were telling the truth. Which meant there had to be some other explanation for how the Slime Monster got into the alley. Then Alex caught himself. This was what Gaby and Casey *wanted* him to think.

"Oh, I get it," Alex said. "This is more of the joke. You pretended the Slime Monster got away to make it seem like he really followed us."

"No, Alex," Casey insisted. "I really lost it. Where did you find it?"

"In the alley off Lafayette Street, as if you didn't know," Alex retorted.

Gaby sniffed the air. "What's that funny smell?"

Come to think of it, there *was* a strange odor in the air. Sort of like a cross between barbecued chicken and burnt rubber. It felt warm inside Gaby's room, too. Uncomfortably warm.

"There's a fire in the bodega!" Alex cried. He ran for the door, closely followed by Gaby and Casey.

When they reached the store, Alex's father was still yelling into the phone, something about a carburetor. And there weren't any flames or smoke. But something very strange was happening. The Crock-Pot was shaking and bouncing on the table, its lid clattering like chattering teeth. Alex, Gaby, and Casey stopped and stared at it.

"What's happening?" Casey asked.

Before anyone could answer, the lid rose up and hot purple foam slopped over the sides of the pot. Like lava, it poured down onto the table and dripped off the edge, onto the floor.

Gaby started to reach for the cooking pot lid.

"No!" Alex warned. "Don't touch! You could get burned!"

Gaby snatched a pair of oven mitts off the counter and put them on. Then she grabbed the lid of the pot.

"Don't do it!" Alex begged. "Who knows what's under there?"

Gaby was afraid. But her curiosity was even stronger. She lifted the lid and everyone looked inside the pot.

Charred and black, like a piece of overcooked meat, the Slime Monster's head sat in the middle of the rice. His eyes were closed, and his face was twisted in pain, like he'd burned to death. The kids stared at him, feeling sick to their stomachs.

Eduardo Fernandez appeared at the end of the counter. "What's going on here?"

"*Oye, papa!*" Gaby said to her father, pointing at the cooking pot. "*Visto lo que Alex hizo con Casey's Slime Monster!*"

"*Me?*" Alex protested. "I didn't do anything to Casey's Slime Monster."

"You must have taken Gooey Gus from my house last night," Casey said accusingly. "And now he's ruined! I've wanted that Slime Monster for such a long time . . ." Though Casey was trying hard not to cry, tears seeped out of her eyes. This made Alex's father even angrier.

"Alejandro, how could you do such a thing?" he demanded. "You've destroyed someone else's property!"

"You and Jamal have taken this Gotcha thing too far," Gaby added.

"Yeah!" Casey chimed in. "You know you're not supposed to overheat a Slime Monster!"

Alex tried to defend himself. "I didn't overheat it!" he cried, but everyone was too busy yelling to listen. And they were too busy yelling to see what was happening in the cooking pot. There was a hissing sound, soft at first but growing louder,

louder, louder! Steam started to rise

from the pot. Then, as if awakening from a deep sleep, the Slime Monster stirred. His bulging, bloodshot eyes popped open, and he cackled evilly.

Ha ha ha ha ha ha ha ha!

Chapter Five

"**W**oooooo!" Lenni said, sounding like a ghost in a haunted house. "The Slime Monster comes alive! I really like what you're doing with the story," she said, complimenting Gaby.

"Yeah," Casey agreed. "This is getting *so scary!*"

Alex rolled his eyes. "Louder, *louder, louder?* Do you think you could put that in a couple *more* times, Gaby? That is, if Edgar Allan Poe doesn't mind you stealing his words."

Gaby spun around on the desk chair and glared at Alex. "I didn't *steal* his words. I was *inspired* by them."

"I guess you were inspired to blame me for everything, too," Alex shot back. "Why's everyone in the story picking on Alex? It's not his fault the Slime Monster got burned. You got some maniac doll jumping into a cooking pot, and Alex has to take the rap."

"But Alex *did* put him in the pot," Casey pointed out.

Alex pushed Gaby's chair so that she rolled away from the computer.

"Hey!" Gaby protested.

Alex wasn't listening to her. He was scrolling back through the story. He stopped when he reached the part where Alex was sniffing the arroz con pollo. "See!" he said, pointing to the text on the screen. "The last time Alex saw the pot, all it had in it was chicken and rice. Which means the Slime Monster got in there by himself."

Lenni's eyes grew wide. "You mean the Slime Monster was alive *before* he heated up?"

All heads turned to Gaby, who smiled mysteriously. "Only the Slime Monster knows for sure," she answered. The important thing is, he's alive *now*. And the hotter he gets, the stronger he gets."

"But it's not fair!" Alex protested. "Some people are going to think *I* did it."

Gaby rolled her chair back in front of the computer, pushing Alex out of the way. "Get a life, Alex," she said. "It's just a story."

"But it's a story about *me*," Alex insisted. "You're making me look bad. Like, what about the part where you said I was a scaredy-cat?"

"Hey! Hey, you guys!" Lenni said, stepping between Alex and Gaby. "Stop fighting."

"I can't let her get away with this," Alex said. "I demand equal time."

"*You* want to write some of the story?" Casey asked.

Alex nodded. "I have to clear my name. The only problem is, how do I write my way out of the mess Gaby put me in?"

Lenni's face lit up. "Hey!" she said. "That's a great idea!"

The other kids looked at her curiously.

"What?" Gaby asked.

Lenni jumped onto the colorful couch and hugged a bright red pillow to her chest. "That's how we can make the story even better. It'll be like a game. One person will write the characters into a dangerous situation, then the next person has to write them out of it."

"That makes it harder to write," Alex pointed out.

"But it makes the story better," Lenni explained. "This way we're creating *obstacles*. You know, problems for the character to solve."

Casey nodded. "That *would* make it more exciting. If they just moseyed along and nothing much happened to them, it would be a pretty boring story."

"Okay," Alex said. "You sold me. Out!" he commanded Gaby, pointing to the desk chair.

Reluctantly, Gaby got up and went to sit on the couch next to Lenni. "My brother's so bossy," she complained. "No wonder he came out that way in my story."

Alex sat down. "Okay," he said. "It's time *Alex*

got to be the hero of the story." He started typing with quick, hard strokes:

The Slime Monster had come alive!

Meanwhile, everyone continued to blame Alex, but he was, is, and always will be . . . cool.

"You had no right to hurt my Slime Monster!" Casey yelled at him.

"Cool," Alex said.

"Yeah, Alex," Gaby complained in her whiny little voice. "Didn't you read the warning on his back? It says 'Do not overheat!' "

"Cool," Alex said. Alex had a secret for keeping calm around his sister. Whenever she started to talk, he played some music in his head, real loud, like a song he'd heard on the radio. Then all he had to do was watch her mouth flapping.

But the music stopped when Alex's father spoke. "You've ruined the arroz con pollo, too," he said. "We can't serve it to customers now."

"Cool," Alex said. [In case you ever read this, Papa, I just want to say that I'd never disrespect you like that in real life. But this is a story, so I can write whatever I want. So don't dock my allowance or anything.]

"Alejandro, I want you to clean up this mess right now," his father told him. "I'll be in the kitchen, cooking another pot of rice."

"No biggie," Alex said. "I'll have this mess cleaned up in no time."

After his father was gone, Alex picked up the lid of the cooking pot. He didn't need gloves like his sister because he wasn't afraid of getting burned. The brave Alejandro felt no pain!

But when Alex lifted up the lid, even he could not believe his eyes. The Slime Monster was gone!

Alex turned triumphantly to his sister. "You see," he declared. "I had nothing to do with this. I was standing here the whole time."

Gaby, for once, was having trouble talking. "Then—how—how did he—"

The girls stared up at Alex as they all realized what was going on. The Slime Monster was alive!

"Oh no!" Casey wailed. "That must be what happens when he overheats!"

Gaby's skinny legs were shaking with fear. "But where did he go?" she asked. "We have to find him right away!"

"Yeah," Alex agreed, taking charge. "He could go around the city, sliming people to death! We have to stop him before it's too late!"

Alex searched the bodega for clues about where the Slime Monster went. He knew all about following clues and solving mysteries. Even before he'd joined the Ghostwriter Team, he'd read dozens of mystery stories. He could always figure out whodunit before the detective in the story did.

So now, Alex looked in the logical place. He started at the cooking pot, where they'd last seen their suspect. There was a big hole in the rice where the Slime Monster's body had been, and some blackened slime that was still bubbling a little. More slime was on the table and the floor. The slime led through the bodega, past the counter, and right out the door. Alex guessed that they'd find more slime if they followed the trail.

"We're on the case!" Alex said, heading for the door. The girls followed him.

Before they got outside, Gaby stepped right into a puddle of purple slime. It was so sticky, she couldn't lift her foot off the floor.

"Yuck!" Gaby exclaimed. Grunting and struggling, she finally got her shoe out of the slime, and they all ran out the door.

Stopping beneath the awning outside the bodega, Alex looked around. On either side of him, colorful fruits and vegetables were stacked in wooden bins. Cars and delivery trucks made their way slowly down Cumberland Street past stores and apartment houses. There was a pool of oil in the middle of the street. There was a melting lump of ice cream on the sidewalk where someone had dropped it. But Alex didn't see any slime.

A ring of steam, blowing up around the edges of a manhole cover, caught Alex's eye. When the steam cleared, Alex saw what he'd been looking for; a big, glistening plop of purple slime. And where there was slime, there was Gooey Gus.

"Hey, guys!" Alex said, pointing. He and the girls ran to the manhole cover. More steam was rising around the rim, but there was no sign of the Slime Monster.

"Gone," Casey said in frustration. "But at least we know he was here."

"The question," Gaby said, "is where is he *now*?"

"I don't know," Alex admitted, "but I'm beginning to see a pattern. First the Crock-Pot, then the steam . . . the Slime Monster's looking for places that are hot!"

"Because heat makes him stronger!" Casey declared.

"Yes!" Alex said. "He must be trying to build his strength so that he can take over the planet!"

The girls cowered, afraid, but not Alex. "Never fear!" he said boldly. "The brave Alejandro is here! I laugh in the face of danger. Ha! Ha! Ha!"

Gaby and Casey looked up at Alex with admiration.

"Wow, big brother," Gaby said. "I feel so much better with *you* here."

With his laser-sharp vision, Alex scanned Cumberland Street. Down the block, he saw a streak of purple on the hood of a parked car. "That way!" he guided them.

Alex ran so fast it was hard for the others to keep up. Perhaps if they'd known what was behind them, they would have moved faster. Over the sound of cars honking and sirens wailing, they couldn't hear the squish, squish, squish of tiny footsteps.

Alex paused by the slime on the car hood. The metal was warm from sitting in the sun. "You see?" he said to the girls. "The car is hot, too. The Slime Monster's definitely heading in this direction." He and the girls continued down the block, little realizing that *they* were the ones being followed.

Squish, squish, squish, squish.

Alex and the girls passed a chain-link fence. Alex paused to sniff the air. With his supersensitive nose, he could smell a basketball sitting nearby, just waiting for a superstud athlete like himself to shoot a few hoops. He looked around. Sure enough, the bright orange basketball was lying on the blacktop on the other side of the fence. Above the basketball, a hoop was calling his name.

"I'll be right back," Alex said, running through the opening in the fence.

The basketball practically leaped into Alex's waiting hands. And once it got there, it was like magic. He dribbled, he dunked, he scored! If this were a basketball story, I'd tell you more, but meanwhile . . .

Gaby and Casey had come upon another pile of purple goo sitting on a corner of the sidewalk.

"We're getting warm," Gaby said. "I can feel it."

She didn't realize how right she was. Two bloodshot eyes, way down near the ground, were staring up at her from behind a garbage can. And a twisted mind was thinking evil thoughts.

Casey stopped to get a better look at the slime. "Looks like it's made of bubble gum," she said, reaching toward it.

"I wouldn't touch it if I were you," Gaby warned.

But Casey wasn't the one in danger. Gaby was. Before she knew what was happening, a stream of slime spewed toward her sneakers, engulfing them.

"Aaaaaaaaaah!" Gaby screamed. Ignoring her own advice, she reached down, trying to pull the slime off her feet and ankles. That was a big mistake. Her hands were instantly fused with her feet, turning her into a giant, upside-down triangle. She couldn't run, she couldn't hide, she couldn't even hop. That's when the Slime Monster made his move.

With incredible strength for such a short guy, he hefted Gaby up and tossed her into a little red wagon that had been sitting on the playground. Then he grabbed the wagon's handle and made off with Gaby at high speed.

"Alex!" Gaby cried. Her hands and feet might have been stuck, but her mouth was still moving.

Alex "Oxygen" Fernandez had just made a superhuman slam-dunk shot, floating for several seconds in the air before coming to a landing. That's when he heard his sister's cry for help. Faster than a thought, Alex arrived on the corner. Casey was standing there, as if frozen, staring down at a pile of slime. In the middle of it was a pair of Gaby-sized footprints. There was no need for Casey to explain.

"Which way did they go?" Alex asked Casey.

Casey pointed down the sidewalk. Moving fast, the Slime Monster was dragging Gaby away in the little red wagon. As he trucked along, he muttered, "I'm *burning* mad! I'm *steaming* mad!" Gaby screamed in terror.

The brave Alejandro ran swiftly, like a panther, pursuing his helpless baby sister and her slimy kidnapper. Sure, Gaby was a pain in the neck. Sure, she was always listening in on his phone calls and borrowing his flannel shirts without asking. Come to think of it, maybe he *wouldn't* save her. But that would have violated his code of honor. The brave Alejandro had to right this wrong, battle evil, and save the innocent, even if the innocent happened to be his sister.

Alex followed the Slime Monster into Prospect Park, where the Evil Dripping One dragged the wagon into a deep thicket of trees. Branches tore at his clothing and scratched his face as he ran through the woods, but Alejandro felt no pain.

At last, Alex emerged from the trees onto a sandy shore. In front of him was a rippling lake, and on the lake a paddleboat. The boat was being rapidly pedaled away by a pair of busy purple feet.

Gaby and the wagon had been dumped in the

back of the boat like a pile of old clothes. She screamed in terror. "Help me, Alex!"

Now she had even more reason to be afraid. The bubble-gum slime was spreading. It had already covered her legs, and it was creeping higher and higher. Soon it would reach her mouth, silencing her forever.

Chapter Six

"**H**ey!" Alex said, smiling at the computer. "I sort of like that idea. Gaby Fernandez, silenced forever."

Gaby poked her brother. "Alex!"

"Just kidding," Alex said.

Knock, knock, knock.

Lenni opened the front door of the loft to Tina Nguyen and Jamal Jenkins. Tina was eleven, and she'd just finished sixth grade at Hurston Middle School. She had shiny, long black hair, which was pulled back with a red barrette. She wore a red-and-white plaid jumper over a long-sleeved black shirt and thigh-high white stockings. Tina was always putting together cool outfits. And she was almost always carrying a video camera on her shoulder. She was probably going to end up shooting movies someday. Today, though, Tina had left her camera at home.

"Look who I ran into on my way here," Tina said, putting her arm around Jamal's shoulders.

Jamal wasn't very tall, but he had a muscular build from all the years he'd been studying karate. He was always calm and steady, even when things got crazy. Jamal was smart, too. He'd been accepted to the High School of Science, where he'd be going next fall.

"You ready to listen to tapes for your party?" Lenni asked Tina.

Tina and Jamal grinned at each other.

"What?" Lenni asked.

"Tina had a great idea while we were walking over here," Jamal said.

"*Me?*" Tina asked. "You're the one who suggested it."

"What is it?" Lenni asked in exasperation.

"Well," Tina began, "we were thinking how much better *live* music is than taped, especially if you want to get people up and dancing . . ."

". . . and then I thought maybe you and Tuan would want to play together on Sunday at Tina's party," Jamal finished, grinning at Lenni.

Tina's brother, Tuan, was sixteen and played guitar for a grunge rock band, the Leaping Dogs. Lenni and Tina had gone to hear them a couple of times and Lenni liked their sound. But grunge rock was so far from her style, it was as if it were from another planet. Not to mention the fact that Tuan was totally obnoxious. He swaggered around with his ripped jeans and beat-up guitar case like he was doing people a favor just by talking to them.

On the other hand, Lenni had been working on a new song about graduation and missing friends. The party would be a great place to play it. And her father always said you had to stretch yourself if you wanted to grow as an artist.

"I'll give it a shot," Lenni said, at last.

"Great," Tina said, heading for the phone. "I'll set the whole thing up."

Jamal wandered over to the computer, where Alex was scrolling through a long piece of text.

"What's up, guys?" Jamal asked.

"We're writing a scary story for the Slime Monster contest," Casey told her cousin. "Everybody's adding a piece. You want to read what we've got so far?"

"Sorry, Casey," Jamal said. "I've got specific orders from Grandma CeCe to bring you straight home. You've got a dentist appointment, remember?"

Casey pouted. "Oh, yeah."

Lenni joined the group at the computer. "Tuan's coming over so we can practice for the party. I guess we'll have to pick up the story tomorrow."

"Awwww," Alex complained. "I was just getting to the good part."

"Buzz-kill," Gaby grumbled. "I wanted to see if the bubble gum was going to eat me alive."

"And what about the deadline?" Casey added. "We'll never finish the story in time if we stop now!"

"Tell you what, little cuz," Jamal said. "Why don't we head over to our house and write the story on *my* computer?"

"Excellent thought, bro," Alex said. "Can I call Hector and see if he wants to come?"

"Sure," Jamal said.

A few minutes later, Alex was sitting in front of the computer in Jamal's bedroom. The ceiling was covered with posters of planets and martial arts movie stars and Dr. Martin Luther King, Jr. A big wooden desk held Jamal's computer.

Nine-year-old Hector Carrero was slowly reading the story on the computer. He had a little trouble with English. His first language was Spanish which he could read and write extremely well. Hector had been born in the United States but, soon after, moved to Puerto Rico to live with his mother and his grandparents. He'd moved back to Brooklyn only a few years ago. Hector was short and skinny with glossy black hair and an olive complexion.

"This is a great story, guys," Hector said. "But how's Alex going to save Gaby?"

"Yeah," Gaby said to Alex. "You're not gonna turn me into a giant wad of bubble gum, are you?"

"Nah," Alex said. "The brave Alejandro will save you, never fear."

"But how's he gonna get across the lake?" Jamal asked.

"I already thought of that," Alex answered. "He's

gonna find a bridge and run across at superspeed."

"But that's too easy," Gaby complained. "What about obstacles? We've got to make it harder for him to get across the water."

Alex sighed. "Okay, okay. Then how 'bout Alex *swims* across at superspeed?"

"Not in the lake at Prospect Park," Hector said. "They've got No Swimming signs up all over the place 'cause the lake's full of weeds you can get tangled up in."

"So what?" Alex asked. "This is a story. I can make up anything I want."

Hector wasn't convinced. "Look," he said, "even if you *were* allowed to swim there, there's no way Alex could catch up with a boat by swimming. It's just not realistic."

Alex got up from the chair in front of the computer and gestured for Hector to sit down. "Okay," he said. "What do you think the Alex in the story would do to save Gaby?"

Hector hesitated. "I don't really know how to type," he said, sitting down, "but I'll try."

Poking at the keys with one finger, Hector typed:

Alex swung on a jungle vine

"You think *that's* more realistic?" Alex asked Hector, laughing. "How's a jungle vine gonna suddenly show up in the middle of Prospect Park?"

Hector shrugged. "I tried."

"Meanwhile," Gaby said, "the gum is creeping up to my armpits. How are we gonna save me? There's got to be some way."

Ghostwriter flashed onto the computer and started typing a message:

What if Alex made a raft and used it to cross the lake?

"Yeah!" Alex said. "Like Tom Sawyer!"

Gaby pursed her lips. "It takes *days* to build a raft, Alex. By the time you got to me, I'd be a giant grape bubble-gum fossil."

"I've got it," Hector said. "What if Alex gets a big pump and empties all the water from the lake so he can run across?"

"Where'd he put all that water?" Jamal asked. "And what would happen to the fish?"

"Yeah," Gaby chimed in. "We can't write a story that's cruel to fish!"

Alex covered his face with his hands. "I give up!" he cried. "It looks like this obstacle's too big to get around."

Ghostwriter must have felt Alex's despair. He typed another message on the computer:

Put me in the story. I'll help Alex save Gaby.

"That's a great idea," Alex said, "but there's a problem. How's the Slime Monster going to *see* Ghostwriter? We're the only ones who can."

"It's a story," Hector argued. "We can write it so the Slime Monster *can* see Ghostwriter."

"There's another problem," Jamal said. "We all promised not to tell anyone about Ghostwriter. We can't just give away the secret."

"But it *wouldn't* be giving anything away," Gaby said. "People who read the story will think we made it up the way we made up the rest of the story."

"Okay," Alex agreed. "It's Ghostwriter to the rescue." He took Hector's place at the computer and started to type:

Alex didn't know how he was going to save his sister. He was beginning to lose hope when, all of a sudden, a bright ball of light streaked through the air like a comet. Alex smiled. "Ghostwriter!"

A superhero like Alex needed a super-sidekick. And that's exactly what Ghostwriter was. He was a ghost who could fly all over the place and read words. Ghostwriter flew past Alex into some bushes near the water's edge. Alex followed and pulled the branches aside. Parked in the sand was a blue plastic paddleboat. Ghostwriter glowed on a name on the side of the boat: S.S. *Minnough.* Ghostwriter had found Alex a boat! Now Alex had a way to save his sister.

"Thanks, Ghostwriter," Alex said. He dragged the boat into the water and hopped in.

Alex's feet were a blur as he pedaled after Gaby at superspeed. But as fast as he was going, the bubble gum was creeping up even faster on Gaby. The festering purple slime had reached all the way to her shoulders. Slimy tentacles oozed up farther, licking around her neck. She turned her face away in terror.

"Hurry, Alex!" she screamed. It was getting difficult for her to breathe. The slime that covered her had begun to harden, like a cement cocoon.

When Alex finally landed on the other side of the lake, Gaby was nowhere in sight. Then Ghostwriter blazed by, leaving a trail of sparkling light. Alex followed Ghostwriter, hoping he would lead him to Gaby.

Ghostwriter darted up a curving path and into a dark tunnel beneath a stone bridge. Alex ran after him.

Drip, drip, drip.

The darkness swam like black milk in front of Alex's eyes. Stumbling over the uneven stones beneath his feet, Alex made his way slowly forward. He listened for his sister's voice, or even the crazed mutterings of the Slime Monster. But the only sound Alex could hear was the eerie *drip, drip, drip* of water leaking down the walls of the tunnel.

"Gaby?" Alex called. "Can you hear me?"

Drip, drip, drip was the only answer.

Was it too late? Had the slime already swallowed his sister up in its deathly embrace?

"*Gaby!*" Alex pleaded. "Please answer!"

Up ahead, a faint purple glow illuminated the tunnel. The walls were shiny with dripping water, and dirty puddles covered the ground ahead of

Alex. Every few seconds, a tiny dark creature would dart from one side of the tunnel to the other. Rats!

Ghostwriter flew toward Alex from the lighted end of the tunnel, circled Alex's head, then flew back to where he'd come from. Dodging puddles and rodents, Alex followed Ghostwriter until they came to a brighter section of the tunnel. It was brighter because there was glowing writing on the wall, letters of purple slime that dripped as ominously as the words they spelled:

Slime, anyone?

The words glowed even brighter as Ghostwriter read them. Then Ghostwriter dropped beneath the letters to a big blobby thing lying on something. Alex stepped closer to get a good look in the dim light. It was roughly triangular in shape, hard and purple, and it pulsed ever so slightly in a regular rhythm. It was lying in a wagon.

A cold chill gripped Alex's heart as he realized what he was looking at. This purple blob was all that was left of his sister, Gaby.

Chapter Seven

It *was* too late! The slime had swallowed Gaby completely. Alex knelt by his sister and wept—yes, wept. He was brave, he was a superhero, but he was not ashamed to show his emotions. Gone was the little sister he'd once shared a room with, read to, helped with her homework. It had been such a short life. Tragically short. Alex's tears dripped like the water in the cave, falling onto the hardened lump that had been his sister.

Then Alex noticed the pulsing. The slime stretched upward for a few seconds, then fell back down again. Up and down. Up and down. It reminded Alex of the rise and fall of a person's chest when they are . . . *breathing!* Gaby was still breathing! That meant she was alive!

"Gaby!" Alex cried joyfully. Then he said something he never thought he'd say in his entire life. "Gaby, say something!"

"Mphmmppm!" said the slime wad. A giant purple bubble rose slowly out of the lump and popped, revealing a mouth beneath. The slime seemed softer around her face. Maybe he could pry it off her. Alex started to reach for his sister.

Gaby said something in a sharp tone, but Alex couldn't quite make out the words.

"What did you say?" he asked.

Another bubble rose from Gaby's lips and popped. "I said, 'Don't touch!' " she repeated, more clearly this time. "Once the bubble gum touches you, it keeps growing till it covers your whole body. And once it hardens, it never comes off!"

Alex wheeled his chair back from the computer and smiled in satisfaction. He'd not only written one whopper of a scary story, he'd also set up a major obstacle for the next writer.

"Wow, Alex," Hector said admiringly. "How are you going to save Gaby?"

"I'm not," Alex said proudly. He looked up at Jamal. "Write your way out of *this* one!"

"Yeah!" Gaby chimed in. "Rock-solid bubble gum that never comes off. That's tough!"

Jamal raised one eyebrow, the way he'd seen Mr. Spock do on the original *Star Trek* TV series. It had taken him months of practice to make it look natural. There was no need to panic merely because he didn't have the slightest idea how to save Gaby. Jamal was confident his logical, scientific mind could solve the problem.

There was the sound of feet stomping up the stairs, and the door to Jamal's bedroom flew open. Casey burst into the room. "I'm back from the dentist!" she announced. "What did I miss?"

Everyone quickly filled Casey in on the story and explained how the next writer had to find a way to free Gaby from her bubble-gum cocoon.

"Nothing's impossible," Jamal said calmly. "In fact, I already have a solution."

Jamal sat down at the computer. "What if we dip Gaby in paint thinner?" he asked as he started to type.

Gaby gasped. "No way! That's too dangerous!"

"But it might dissolve the gum," Alex argued.

Gaby emphatically shook her head. "It might dissolve me, too!"

Jamal deleted the line about paint thinner and stared thoughtfully into the computer screen. "How to unstick gum . . . ," he said softly. "How to unstick gum . . ." Then Jamal punched his right fist into the palm of his left hand. "Aha!" he exclaimed. He saved the document.

"What are you doing?" Alex asked him.

Jamal got up from his chair. "I need to do some research," he said, heading out the door.

The other kids looked at each other, mystified. Then Casey noticed something stranger. Her Slime Monster doll, now wearing a woolen cap and mittens, was sitting on top of Jamal's desk lamp. He looked nice and toasty warm.

"Hey!" she called, pointing at the action figure. "Who did that to him?"

The others shrugged.

Casey's eyes narrowed. "Oh, I get it. Someone's playing a joke, right? Making it look like the Slime Monster's trying to heat himself up just like in the story."

No one said anything.

Casey considered herself a down-to-earth girl who knew the difference between real and make-believe. The story the team was writing was definitely make-believe. Slime Monsters didn't come alive, they didn't go running around the neighborhood jumping into Crock-Pots or dragging kids away in little red wagons. *Her* Slime Monster, the *real* Slime Monster, was just a plastic doll with batteries in its stomach. *Her* Slime Monster couldn't move by itself.

Still, Casey couldn't help thinking about the warning printed on the Slime Monster: DO NOT OVERHEAT. Why would the company put that on the toy if there was nothing to worry about? She stole a look at the Slime Monster cozied up to the seventy-five-watt lightbulb. The Slime Monster was grinning evilly.

Casey was about to say something when Jamal came striding back into the room carrying a book: *Helena's Helpful Hints.*

"What's that for?" Gaby asked.

Jamal sat down in front of the computer. "Grandma CeCe uses this all the time," he explained as he flipped through the pages. "It's got solutions to common household problems. Stains that won't come out, how to recycle egg cartons . . ."

"You think there's something in there about unsticking gum?" Hector asked.

"That's what I'm hoping," Jamal said. "I'll look under *B* for *Bubble Gum.*" When he found the right page, everyone looked over his shoulder. Ghostwriter read along with the rest of the team, glowing over the words:

Helena's Helpful Hints
BUBBLE GUM, How to remove: *Rub the area with ice until gum hardens. Then remove by scraping it off.*

"That's it!" Jamal cried, snapping the book shut. "That's how we're going to save Gaby!" He put the book down.

"What's he gonna do?" Casey wondered aloud.

"Probably something cool," Gaby guessed.

Jamal smiled. "You mean, something *cold,*" he said as he started to type:

Jamal, the peaceful warrior, stood very still in his living room. He was emptying his mind of all thoughts as he prepared to battle his imaginary opponent. Bowing to show his respect, he launched into his kata, a series of karate blocks, kicks, and punches. By practicing these moves over and over again, he was making them instinctive in case he ever needed to use them in a real-life battle.

He wore loose-fitting white cotton pants tied at the waist with a black belt, which was tattered from many years of training. His bare torso glistened with sweat, his muscles seemed sculpted out of marble. Turning to the left, he did a down-block against an imaginary kick to the ribs. Then he punched with his tightly clenched right fist into his opponent's—

A knock at the door interrupted his concentration. Ordinarily, Jamal didn't let anything get in the way of his karate training. But his finely tuned senses detected danger. Jamal bowed once again to his imaginary opponent, then strode toward the door and opened it.

Alex was there, looking desperate and afraid. "Jamal!" he said, clutching his friend's arm. "You gotta help me! Gaby's been slimed!"

Alex always did have a tendency to overreact. Jamal tried to calm him with his own inner peace. "Relax," Jamal advised him. "Empty your mind of all thoughts."

"There's no time!" Alex shouted, trying to pull Jamal out the door. "We gotta save her! Come on!"

Moments later, Jamal and Alex wheeled the little red wagon into the living room with the Gaby chunk loaded on it. While Alex circled the wagon, wringing his hands in despair, Jamal studied the hardened gum with a cool eye. Gaby was still breathing. That was a good sign. But they couldn't touch the gum to pull it off her because they'd get slimed, too. There had to be a way to get the gum off without harming Gaby or themselves.

The correct answer suddenly came to Jamal. "Ice!" he said.

Alex looked perplexed. "Ice?"

"Of course," Jamal said. "If we rub some ice on the gum, it will freeze. Then we can scrape the gum off."

"Wow, Jamal," Alex said, impressed. "How'd you know that?"

Jamal smiled modestly. "Natural brilliance."

Fortunately, Alex had access to plenty of ice because his father stocked it at the bodega. The boys ran to get some. Quickly returning to Jamal's house, they laid the freezing-cold bags all over the bubble-gum shell that entrapped Gaby. Jamal could only imagine the fear the young girl must have felt inside, alone, surrounded by darkness, struggling for breath. He didn't know if she could hear him, but he tried to reassure her.

"We're gonna get you out of there," he promised.

After several moments, Jamal was beginning to notice surface changes on the hardened bubble gum. The ice had turned it from dark purple to light, and countless small cracks ran through it like veins. This was a good sign. It meant the substance was becoming more brittle. It was time for the next part of his plan.

Jamal ran down to the basement and found his father's tool chest. He pulled out a hammer and chisel. Jamal returned to the living room, stopping first in the kitchen to get a pair of rubber gloves. Fully equipped now, he put on the yellow gloves and carefully tried to chip away at the bubble-gum cocoon.

Nothing happened.

"It's not working!" Alex wailed, pacing back and forth on the carpet. "The gum's too hard!"

Patience had never been Alex's strong point. Jamal kept banging away with the hammer and chisel. But after ten more minutes, he was forced to conclude that Alex was right. To free Gaby, a more powerful force was necessary.

Flinging away the hammer and chisel, Jamal stared down at the cocoon with intense concentration. He emptied his mind of all thoughts. Then he raised his right gloved hand high into the air. His fingers were straight and stiff and pressed closely together. This was called "knife hand," one of karate's most effective weapons.

With an earth-shattering cry, Jamal's knife hand struck the cocoon. Instantly, it broke apart, and Gaby popped up like a chick hatching from its shell.

"Jamal!" she sobbed, throwing her arms around his shoulders. "You saved me!"

Jamal patted Gaby's back in a fatherly manner. He was no hero, really. Just a simple man trying to do good in an evil world. Still, Gaby clung to him in gratitude.

"Hey!" Alex said jealously to his sister. "What about me?"

"Thanks for getting Jamal, Alex," Gaby said. "That was good thinking."

Jamal now turned his attention to the frozen slime. Several small pieces had broken off and were lying on the carpet. Since he was still wearing rubber gloves, Jamal decided it would be safe to pick up a piece of slime to get a closer look.

The frozen slime fragment looked like thousands of tiny pieces of frosty lavender glass all stuck together. "Fascinating," Jamal said. "Alex, Gaby, take a look at this."

As the three gathered around the frozen specimen, a pair of slimy purple feet silently descended the stairs.

"I'd like to examine this under my microscope," Jamal said.

Alex looked fearful. "Are you sure it's safe to keep this stuff around?"

"I'll keep it frozen," Jamal promised. "It may help us figure out how to defeat the Slime Monster."

The slimy purple feet shuffled across the living room carpet.

"He's out there somewhere," Gaby said, looking out the window. "And we've got to catch him before he—"

A slimy purple hand reached out from under the sofa and grabbed Alex's ankle.

"Slime, anyone?" the gruff voice asked.

"Aaaaaaaah!" Alex screamed. He shook his ankle with all his might, but the little purple creature held on tight. Alex didn't dare use his hands to pry the monster off, because then he'd end up completely slimed, like Gaby.

"We've got to save Alex!" Gaby shouted, kicking at the monster every time Alex's flailing leg came her way.

Alex fought desperately, trying to free himself from the Slime Monster's clutches, but he was beginning to tire. The creature's mouth filled with the deadly purple poison as it got ready to spit at Alex's leg.

Chapter Eight

Jamal spun around in his chair and faced Hector. "Alex is about to become the Slime Monster's next victim," he said in a deep, ominous voice. "How are you going to get him out of *that*?"

Hector's thin face froze. "Me?"

Alex patted Hector on the back. "Yeah, Hector!" he said. "It's your turn."

Hector's face was pale and he wrapped his arms around himself.

Ghostwriter must have felt Hector's fear because he flew into the computer and wrote rapidly on the monitor.

You write great stories, Hector.

Hector shook his head.

"Ghostwriter's right," Alex said. "You do write great stories. Like the one you wrote about playing handball in the rain."

"That's different," Hector said. "Those things really happened to me."

"Well, just make believe the Slime Monster is really after us," Casey suggested. "And write whatever comes out."

"But I don't spell too good, and I can't type, either," Hector resisted.

"I'll type it for you," Jamal volunteered. "You just talk, and I'll write down what you say."

"Okay," Hector said slowly. "But I need some time to think about this. Can we pick this up again tomorrow?"

"Agreed," Jamal said. "It's time for dinner, anyway."

Casey looked around the room. "Hey!" she said. "What happened to the Slime Monster?"

Everyone looked at the lamp on Jamal's desk. The Slime Monster wasn't there.

If someone was playing a joke, Casey didn't think it was very funny. But how could someone have taken the Slime Monster from the room? They'd all been there the whole time. On the other hand, they'd all been so busy reading while Jamal was typing that maybe someone could have snuck the action figure away.

"I'd like my Slime Monster, please," Casey said firmly.

"I don't have it," Gaby said, holding up her empty hands.

"Me neither," Alex said.

Jamal shrugged and held up his empty hands. "Don't look at me. I was typing the whole time."

"I was sitting right next to you," Hector said.

Casey forced a smile. "Okay. Whoever did it, ha ha ha. Just make sure you give it back when you're done, okay?"

After everyone had left and Jamal had gone downstairs for dinner, Casey tiptoed back into her cousin's room and looked around. She checked under the bed. She searched all his desk and dresser drawers. She shook his pillow and lifted up the rug.

"Gus?" she called nervously. "Are you in here?"

Creak!

Was that a footstep or just the floorboards settling in the summer heat? Casey didn't wait to find out. She slammed the door behind her, ran into her bedroom, and hid under the covers.

Early Saturday morning, the team reassembled in Jamal's room. Lenni wasn't there because she was rehearsing for the party with Tuan, but Tina had stopped by to see how the story was going. Hector reached into the pocket of his baggy shorts and pulled out a piece of notebook paper that had been folded and folded until it was the size of a quarter.

"Okay," Hector said, unfolding the paper. It was covered with scribbled words in English and Spanish and drawings that looked like a rough comic strip. "I'm gonna get Alex and Gaby and Jamal out of this mess." He cleared his throat and glanced at the paper where he'd written his ideas. Then he began to speak.

"Alex was scared to death," Hector said, sounding sort of scared himself. "He kicked his leg to shake off the Slime Monster."

Jamal typed rapidly on the computer, trying to keep up with Hector:

Alex was scared to death. He kicked his leg to shake off the Slime Monster.

"Get off me!" Alex shouted real loud.

But the monster wouldn't let go. "I'm *burning* mad! I'm *steaming* mad!" it said.

Alex was getting pretty tired of this. He had to lose this creepy monster once and for all. Alex gave one big kick of his foot and *whoosh*! The Slime Monster went flying across the room. It hit the wall and slid down to the carpet. Then it scurried across the room like a rat, right to where Jamal, Alex, and Gaby were standing.

"Let's get out of here!" Gaby said.

All three of them ran to the front door. But when they got there, who did they see grinning up at them? You guessed it. El Slimo. They couldn't get out that way, so they ran for the kitchen. There was a back door out the kitchen they could take. But when they got to the kitchen door, Gooey Gus was waiting for them again.

"The window!" Jamal said, and they all ran that way. But when they got to the window, there was the Lime Monster, grinning like the evil thing he was.

"You laughing at me?" he growled. "You laughing at *me*?"

A muffled giggle behind him made Hector turn around. Casey had covered her mouth with both hands, and her chest was heaving up and down.

"Are you laughing at me?" Hector asked, upset. "I guess it was stupid for me to try to write something. I can't do it as good as the rest of you."

Casey shook her head and pointed to the screen. "I'm not laughing at your story, Hector. Your story's great! But look what Jamal typed!"

Hector hadn't been paying any attention to the computer monitor, but now he glanced over Jamal's shoulder. Then he saw the mistake.

"*Lime* Monster?" he asked Jamal, laughing himself.

Jamal peered at the screen. "Oops!" Then he fixed his dark-brown eyes on Hector. "Could you talk a little slower, maybe?" he asked. "I'm having trouble keeping up with you."

"Sure," Hector said, feeling more confident now. Casey liked his story, and it seemed as if the other kids did, too. While Jamal added an *S* in front of *lime*, Hector started talking again.

"So the kids were stuck . . ."

So the kids were stuck. Whichever way they went, there was the Slime Monster ready to slime them to death. They had to get out of there.

"I got it!" said Jamal, pounding his right fist into the palm of his left hand. He did that a lot, but it was okay because it usually meant he had a good idea. "Gooey Gus can't block all the exits at the same time," Jamal said. "Let's split up."

Gaby said, "I'll call a rally in my room. We've gotta find a way to stop the Slime Monster before he slimes us to death! But first I want to take a shower and wash this disgusting slime off me. It feels like dead, squishy worms rubbed all over my skin!"

Gaby pulled her Ghostwriter pen from around her neck and wrote "Rally G" on her hand. A rally was a meeting for the entire Ghostwriter Team to get cracking on a case. Ghostwriter read Gaby's message and flew out the window to tell the rest of the team.

"Okay," Jamal said. "On the count of three. One, two, three!"

Alex ran for the front door, Gaby ran for the back door, and Jamal ran down the basement stairs because there was another door out that way. And Jamal was right. The Slime Monster couldn't follow them all. But that was okay with the Slime Monster. He had a *bigger* plan in mind.

Meanwhile, the kids ran to the bodega and met

in Gaby's room. And with their friend Hector on the case, they had a much better chance. Hector was the boss, now, and he knew exactly what to do. He marched up and down the room while the team sat on Gaby's bed and listened with deep respect.

Hector had it all worked out. First, they had to figure out where the Slime Monster went. And second, they had to find a way to stop him *para siempre*—for good. No more Slime Monster! But they had to watch their own backs because the Slime Monster could sneak up on them again!

Hector figured the Slime Monster was still hanging out in hot places, so he made a list of all the different spots in the neighborhood that were hot, like pizza ovens, and toasters and clothes dryers and steam pipes running underground. The kids thought Hector was on to something, so they all split up to search the neighborhood. Except Jamal. He went home to look at the slime under his microscope. He was hoping that would help him figure out a way to put the Slime Monster out of business for good!

As everybody left the bodega, they gave Hector a sharp salute. He saluted back and said, "Remember, everybody. Don't let the slime touch your skin!"

The team took Hector's advice. Everybody went home and got stuff to cover themselves up so they wouldn't get slimed. Gaby wore her raincoat and rubber boots and a bicycle helmet. Casey wore an old hockey mask of Jamal's that had one of those clear plastic shields on the front of it. And she wore oven mitts to cover her hands. You get the idea. And they all went out into Brooklyn to find the Slime Monster.

It was a really hot day, the kind where the pavement on the street gets all sticky and the air starts waving back and forth in front of your face. The kind where you're afraid to touch anything made of metal 'cause you could burn the skin off your fingers. In other words, it was the perfect temperature for Gooey Gus. And that's what Casey was thinking as she was walking down the street.

"It's so hot," she said, "that gum wad could be anywhere." She opened up a garbage can and looked inside. Slimy wasn't in there. But then Ghostwriter flew up to her and swirled around on a sticker on the garbage can—you know, one of those stickers they put on for recycling. And when Ghostwriter was done swirling the letters around, he'd spelled out the words: **WARNING: DO NOT OVERHEAT!**

Casey knew what that meant. It meant Ghostwriter had read those words on the Slime Monster, which meant Gooey Gus was probably nearby! But where was he? Casey looked around. He wasn't at the bus stop and he wasn't waiting at the corner for the light to change and he wasn't window-shopping in one of the stores.

Ghostwriter rearranged some more letters on a street sign:

Casey, watch out!

But before Casey could read the warning, a hand stuck up out of the sewer and tried to grab her and pull her down!

Casey screamed. "Aaaaaaaah! Aaaaaaaaaah! Aaaaaaaaaah! Aaaaaaaaaah! Aaaaaaaaaah!" [This is Jamal writing while Hector keeps screaming. I just want to say, "Get on with the story already, Hector. You're going to wake up my grandmother!"]

The Slime Monster spewed all this really thick, smelly, sewer slime all over Casey. I mean, *all* over her! Boy was she glad she'd listened to Hector and put on her protection, 'cause she didn't get a drop on her skin. She was still mad, though. *Burning* mad! She wasn't going to let Gooey Gus get away with this.

Casey looked down into the sewer, but it was dark in there and she couldn't see anything. She knew Gooey Gus was still down there, though, because she could hear him sloshing around in the dirty water.

"I'm gonna get you, Slimy!" she yelled.

When Casey got home, she threw out all her grossed-up slimy clothes and changed into something clean. Then she went downstairs. Jamal was in the living room looking at the frozen slime under his microscope. Gaby was there, too. Casey told them how she'd been slimed and the monster got away. Then she wanted to know if Jamal had found any scientific answers. But before Jamal could answer, his grandmother came running in from the kitchen, screaming her head off.

"Aaaaaah! Aaaaaaaah! Aaaaaaaaah!" [This is Jamal again. I don't want to say anything against Hector's story because I like it, but I wish he wouldn't scream so loud. He's breaking my eardrum! If you're reading this, just assume that Hector keeps screaming while I'm typing. Oh good. He stopped.]

Grandma CeCe was wearing an apron and oven mitts. "There's a horrible creature in my oven!" she shouted. [Jamal here. Hector does a great imitation of my grandmother. Sounds just like her!]

"Was it purple?" Gaby asked. "With bulging eyes?"

Grandma nodded. "And slimy and blobby! Where are the yellow pages? I've got to call an exterminator!"

"No, Grandma," Jamal said. "An exterminator won't be able to get rid of it. Let me try."

Jamal took the mitts and apron from Grandma and the bicycle helmet from Gaby. Then he marched bravely into the kitchen.

"Be careful, Jamal!" Grandma CeCe said.

"I hope he knows what he's doing," Gaby said with fear in her voice.

They heard a scream coming from the kitchen, then Jamal came running out into the living room, clutching his forehead. It was covered with a big fat glob of steaming purple goo. All this smoke rose out of it and there was the smell of burning flesh. Jamal screamed in pain.

"*Aaaaaaah! Aaaaah!*" [etc. etc. etc.]

"He's been slimed!" Casey said.

"Slimed?" Grandma said. She was so shocked, she fainted on the couch.

Meanwhile, Jamal kept screaming. "Owwwww! It's so hot! It's burning my skin off! I can feel it crawling all the way into my brain. *Aaahhhh! Help!*"

Chapter Nine

"*Aaahhhhh!*" Hector screamed while everyone around him held their ears. He wasn't just screaming. He was clutching his face in agony and doubled over, as if in real pain. Hector had been slow to get started with the story, but now he was out of control. "Help!" Hector shouted. "Help!"

Grandma CeCe ran into the room, looking sleepy and confused. She was tall and wide with short graying hair. Everybody in the neighborhood knew who she was because she delivered mail for the post office. "What's going on here?" she asked. "Did somebody get hurt?"

Hector dropped down to the floor and groaned as if he had swallowed a porcupine. "Aaaah! Ooooohhhhh! Eeeeeeeeh!"

The other kids knew Hector had just been acting while he was telling the story, but now they were getting worried.

"Don't just sit there, Jamal," Grandma CeCe snapped at him. "Call an ambulance!"

Hector's eyes closed and he lay very still. Grandma knelt beside him and felt his wrist for a pulse. "Hector?" she asked, nearly hysterical. "Hector?"

All of a sudden, Hector's eyes popped open and he grinned. "Gotcha!"

Everybody laughed except for Grandma CeCe.

"You scared the living daylights out of me!" she told Hector. "You'd better cut out the 'gotcha' before *I* getcha!"

Grandma CeCe started to leave. Before she got into the hallway, Casey called to her. "Hey, Grandma. You seen my Slime Monster? I can't find it anywhere."

Grandma CeCe shook her head. "Sorry, honey. But I'll keep my eyes open."

Casey was starting to worry about her action figure. Everyone knew it was missing and that she wanted it back. And no one on the team would steal her doll or even hide it for such a long time. But Casey refused to believe the Slime Monster had walked out of the room on its own. This was real life, and dolls just didn't do that. Casey's head was beginning to hurt from thinking about it.

"C'mon!" Gaby said. "Let's get back to the story."

"Yeah, Hector," Jamal said. "You can't just leave me hanging! The slime was crawling all the way into my brain."

"I guess I set up a good *obstacle* for the next person." Hector grinned at Tina.

"Yeah, Tina," Alex said. "You haven't gone yet."

Tina looked at her watch. "Sorry, guys. I want to write something, but I promised Lenni and Tuan I'd listen to their new song. I'll come right back as soon as they're done." Tina waved and walked out the door.

Jamal shrugged and looked at Hector. "Guess you're not going to pass this one off so easily."

Hector screwed up his mouth. "Okay," he said, looking down at his creased piece of paper. "I've got some more good stuff right here." Hector pointed to some scribbled words and began telling his part of the story again. "Jamal could feel the burning slime eating into his liver. Then his eyeballs fell out."

"Ech!" Alex exclaimed. "This is great!"

Encouraged, Hector continued as Jamal typed. "The blood came pouring from his eye sockets like rivers . . ."

Gaby looked disgusted. "Ewwww!"

Casey stopped Hector. "Sorry. You can't write that. The contest rules say no blood and no guns."

Jamal deleted the last two sentences.

Hector crossed his arms over his chest and scowled. "No fair," he said. "My job was to do an obstacle for the next person."

"But everybody here's written something already," Alex pointed out.

A flash of light burst out of the computer and words started appearing on the screen.

"Not everybody," Jamal said, smiling. He pushed his chair back and watched as Ghostwriter took over the next part of the story:

Jamal could feel the burning slime eating into his liver.

Gaby ran in with some ice and quickly applied it to Jamal's forehead. Jamal was saved! But the Slime Monster was still at large. Ghostwriter quickly picked up the trail. The air was thick with words and letters: street names, traffic instructions, advertisements for hand cream and fat-free cookies. But far in the distance, way up high, he could see a tiny warning: DO NOT OVERHEAT! Ghostwriter could sense something, too, coming from beneath the words. Anger, vengeance, and a little bit of loneliness.

Ghostwriter was shaken by this. Ordinarily, he could feel emotions coming from his friends: Jamal, Lenni, Alex, Gaby, Tina, Hector, and Casey. There'd been a few other kids along the way, too, but he'd never before been able to sense feelings from a *monster*. What did this mean? Ghostwriter had no answer. He didn't choose whom he could feel. It just happened. Perhaps it was part of some larger plan.

But there was no time for philosophizing. Ghostwriter had to lead his friends to the slime-covered madman. Fixing his mind on the distant warning, Ghostwriter felt the present room slip away. Words flew past him and behind him: The Party Animal, First Federal Savings Bank, Do Not Litter, Do Not Enter, Tung Hoy Chinese Restaurant. Ghostwriter could also feel the presence of Gaby and Casey behind him, moving quickly to keep up with him.

More words swept past. Paris Cleaners, No Parking, Nguyen Tailor Shop. Ghostwriter was entering familiar territory. Tina's parents owned the tailor shop, and their apartment was in the basement of the same building. The warning, now, was directly above him. While Ghostwriter had never actually "seen" Tina's building, he guessed that this meant the Slime Monster must be on the roof.

Ghostwriter could have flown straight up into the air, through floors and ceilings, to get to the roof, but he knew Gaby and Casey did not have this ability. So he searched for a word such as *Staircase*. He found it and flew upward, knowing the girls would understand to follow.

Ghostwriter emerged from the staircase. The DO NOT OVERHEAT was much larger now, and the Slime Monster's presence was far more intense.

Gaby and Casey ran out onto the roof, still wearing their protective gear. The broad, flat roof was covered with a black, sticky tar paper and surrounded by a high brick wall. Every so often, a metal pipe rose up out of the tar paper and wisps of steam puffed gently out.

In a corner of the roof, between two steam pipes, was a small lawn chair. This was not unusual for New York City, as people often used roofs for relaxing and other recreational activities. What was unusual was that the *Slime Monster* was sitting in the lawn chair, sunning himself. He held a reflector up to his face so that the sun's rays shone even more brightly upon him. Gooey Gus grinned with evil pleasure as the sun heated his skin.

"There he is!" Gaby said, pointing to the purple sunbather.

Casey looked, too, and gasped. The Slime Monster's skin was becoming shiny and soft. Bubbles began to rise from his skin: rising, popping, and falling. It was like staring into a vat of boiling wax.

"What's happening?" Casey wondered.

"I'm *burning* mad. I'm *steaming* mad!" the monster said as he began to ooze out of his chair.

"He's getting too hot!" Gaby shouted. "We've got to cool him off!"

Gaby frantically searched the roof for something—anything—she could use. Then her eyes lit upon a bucket of water standing near the stairwell door. Gaby grabbed the bucket and flung the water over the grinning demon. Gooey Gus sank back into his chair and his eyes closed.

"You did it, Gaby!" Casey congratulated her.

The Slime Monster's eyes popped open and he smiled with all three of his teeth.

"Uh-oh," Gaby said worriedly. "Guess that bucket was sitting in the sun too long."

The monster's face, always misshapen, began to shift around. The skin stretched tighter and tighter and his eyes bulged more menacingly. His hands, always large, seemed to grow larger as the fingers lengthened and thickened.

The girls, staring in horror, quickly realized that it was time to go. They ran for the stairway, but before they could reach it, the door slammed shut.

"Slime, anyone?" asked the Slime Monster. His voice sounded deeper than before, and angrier.

Casey and Gaby pulled on the door handle, trying to open it, but the door remained firmly shut.

Slow, squishy footsteps came lumbering up behind them. Gaby was scared to look, but she was even more afraid of what the monster would do behind her back. Timidly, she turned her head. Casey did, too. And what they saw was so horrifying, they couldn't even scream.

The Slime Monster was now six feet tall! Huge and hulking, he came closer and closer. Hot purple droplets dripped from his body and sizzled on the black tar roof. His hands, as big as baseball mitts, were reaching for Gaby and Casey as his mouth filled with poison slime.

Gaby and Casey struggled desperately with the handle of the door. Why wouldn't it open? Casey kicked the door in desperation. Any second now, Gooey Gus would be close enough to slime them to death!

Chapter Ten

"**W**hoa!" Tina exclaimed a few hours later, reading the pages Ghostwriter had written. She'd returned from the rehearsal at Lenni's and was now perched on Jamal's desk. "The monster's six feet tall and my girls are stuck on the roof with no way out!"

Casey grinned. "Leave it to a ghost to write a scary story."

"*And* set up an obstacle for the next person," Hector added.

Ghostwriter quickly typed a message on Jamal's computer:

Tina's turn!

Tina jumped a little. "I know I should be used to it by now, but how'd he know I was here?"

"Ghostwriter always knows," Jamal said, tossing a spongy minibasketball through the hoop on the back of his bedroom door. An electronic crowd cheered.

"Wish he knew where my Slime Monster was," Casey fretted. "I still can't find it."

Tina slipped into the empty chair in front of the computer. "Okay," she said, a determined look on her pretty, round face. "It's time the *girls* got to be brave and fearless."

"Yeah!" Gaby and Casey said at the same time.

Tina began typing as if she already knew exactly what to write:

Any second now, Gooey Gus would be close enough to slime them to death!

Casey and Gaby tugged at the door, trying to *will* it open. But time was running out. The Slime Monster was only inches away, exhaling steam from his uneven nostrils. He rolled the poison slime around in his mouth, getting ready to spit it at the girls. But did they give up? No!

"Come on, Casey," Gaby said, feeling a new surge of courage. "We're strong women. We can do this."

Casey felt her strength return. "Yeah!" she said. She and Gaby grabbed the door handle and, pulling at the same time, gave it a mighty heave. The door burst open, revealing a rectangle of darkness that was the stairwell. The girls ran down the stairs as fast as they could, barely escaping the purple stream of slime that arched out of the monster's mouth.

The monster had been mad when he was only

two feet tall. But now his anger had grown as big as he was. And so had his evil power. The Slime Monster lurched after them with slow, squishy footsteps.

Gaby ran for the only safe place she could think of—home. But when she got to the front door of the bodega, it was locked and there was a sign saying CLOSED. She remembered that her parents had gone to visit friends. That meant no one was around to help them, not her mother or her father or her brother, Alex. This was not an ideal situation, but Gaby and Casey would figure out a way to defend themselves.

"Come on," Gaby said, leading Casey around the building to the back. "We'll hide out in my room until the coast is clear."

Inside Gaby's bedroom, the girls locked the door and dragged the desk in front of it. "That should hold him," Casey said.

BOOM! BOOM! BOOM!

The sound was so close, it made them jump. The Slime Monster was pounding on the bedroom door.

BOOM! BOOM! BOOM!

The wood was starting to splinter from the force of his mighty hand. The door wasn't going to hold for long.

"You laughing at me?" Gooey Gus demanded. "You laughing at *me*?"

"We've got to get out of here!" Gaby said. "And

there's only one other way." Gaby grabbed her desk chair and pulled it across the floor to the gated window. She climbed up on the chair and tried to open the metal gate.

BOOM! BOOM! BOOM!

"Hurry!" Casey shouted, glancing nervously at the door.

Gaby *was* hurrying, but the gate hadn't been opened in years and was caked with rust. And Gaby was so nervous, her fingers were shaking, which didn't make opening the gate easier.

BOOM! A fist the size of a cantaloupe broke through the wooden door. The desk still blocked the exit, but Casey had a feeling it wouldn't for long. Then she heard a creeping, sloshing, slurping sound. What was that? The sound was coming from near her feet.

Casey looked down and saw purple slime sliding toward her feet. The slime actually looked . . . *hungry* . . . like it wanted to eat her alive.

"Gaby!" Casey screamed, running toward the window where Gaby was still rattling the rusted-shut gate.

The slime was picking up speed now. Casey tried to jump up on the chair with Gaby, but there wasn't room for them both.

BOOM! Another punch destroyed what was left of the door. Now only the desk stood between the monster and the girls.

With a reluctant squeak, the window gate finally

gave in to Gaby's tugging fingers. She pulled it across and lifted the window open. It was a tiny window, just large enough for a young girl to pass through.

"Come on, Casey," Gaby urged, boosting herself up on the windowsill and sticking her head and shoulders outside into the alley. Gaby always used to complain about having a bedroom on the ground floor because there was too much noise outside from wailing cats and loud radios and shrill car alarms. But now she was glad her room was so low because it was only a short drop from the window to the street.

Casey tried to climb up on the chair beneath the window, but something was holding her back. She stared down at her feet and screamed. The slime had completely engulfed her sneakers and was holding them fast to the floor.

"My shoes are stuck!" Casey shouted to Gaby in the alley.

"Leave 'em," Gaby shouted back. "If that slime touches your skin, you're a goner!"

Using the chair for leverage, Casey wiggled her feet out of her sneakers. But just as she was climbing up on the chair, there was a huge CRASH! The Slime Monster had shoved the desk aside and burst into the room.

"You laughing at me?" he demanded as he sloshed through his own slime.

Casey wasn't laughing. She was trying to get

out that window as fast as she could. She got one leg over the windowsill, then ducked out backward, pulling her other leg through. Gaby was there to help her down.

Without a word, the girls ran down the alley. The Slime Monster oozed out through the narrow opening in the window and followed right behind them. *SLOSH! SLOSH! SLOSH! SLOSH!*

"We've got to warn the others," Gaby shouted at the end of the alley. "I think I know where Alex is." Hanging a right, Gaby led Casey to the chainlink fence that surrounded the basketball court. Sure enough, there was Alex shooting hoops with Hector.

"Alex!" Gaby screamed as she ran past, followed by Casey in her stockinged feet. *"He's coming!"*

When Alex saw the six-foot Slime Monster sloshing up Lafayette Street, he dropped the basketball. Hector stared with his mouth open. He'd never seen anything that big, or that ugly, in his entire life.

"Slime, anyone?" Gooey Gus boomed in his now deep voice.

Alex and Hector took off running after Gaby and Casey. The four of them zigged and zagged, through parks and driveways and alleys, trying to lose Gus, but it was no use. He was on their trail and wouldn't take no for an answer.

The kids ran past Hurston Middle School, where

Tina was interviewing Jamal with her video camera.

"Tell us what you'll remember most about Hurston," Tina asked as she looked into the eyepiece. Jamal's face was a little out of focus, so she turned the lens until it became clearer. But what was that commotion in the background? A whole bunch of people were running toward them on the sidewalk and screaming. They were making so much noise that Tina couldn't hear Jamal's answer. Tina lowered the camera so that she could ask the people to please be quiet. But as they came closer, Tina realized who they were! Gaby, Alex, Hector, and Casey, who wasn't wearing any shoes!

"What's wrong?" Tina shouted as they ran by.

The answer came stomping up the street after the Ghostwriter Team. The answer was twisted and purple and six feet tall.

"Aaaaah!" Jamal shouted and took off with his friends. Still clutching her camera, Tina ran as fast as she could.

It didn't matter where they went: the subway, the video arcade, or the community center. The monster followed them. He didn't seem interested in anyone else, only them. And he was *burning* for revenge. Finally, the kids ended up back at the bodega, which was still empty.

Fumbling for his key, Alex unlocked the door and the team rushed inside. Alex quickly locked the door behind them. Gaby and Casey, who'd been through this drill before, started dragging boxes in front of the door.

"Good idea," Alex said, helping them. "Let's block the door so the Slime Monster can't get in."

"I'll call the police," Gaby volunteered, running around the counter and picking up the telephone. The receiver felt too light. Gaby looked at it and gasped. The cord that usually connected the receiver to the phone had been cut. Or, to be more accurate, it had been slimed. The severed end of the cord was black and burnt and sticky with purple goo.

Gaby dropped the phone and checked her hands for traces of slime. But before she could feel relieved that her hands were clean, she heard that old, familiar sound at the back door.

BOOM! BOOM! BOOM!

After all that effort to block the front door, Gooey Gus was trying to come in the back!

"We've got to stop him!" Hector cried.

"It's too late," Gaby wailed. "We're gonna be gum balls any minute!"

CRASH!

Just as Gaby had feared, the Slime Monster was breaking down the back door the way he'd broken down the door to her room.

SQUISH! SQUISH! SQUISH! SQUISH!

The Slime Monster was moving a lot faster now that his legs were longer. And he was getting even more touchy. The walls shook at the sound of his voice. "You laughing at me? You laughing at *me*?"

The team cowered in fear as the Slime Monster burst into the bodega.

Chapter
Eleven

"**W**ow, Tina," Casey said enthusiastically. "The way you wrote the story, I can see the whole thing happening!"

Tina looked pleased. "I sort of see it in my head, like a movie. Then I write down what I see."

"Well, keep it up," Alex said encouragingly. "What happens now?"

Tina got up from Jamal's desk chair. "What happens now is I start getting ready for my party. I've got to buy some groceries and help my mother cook the dumplings for tomorrow."

Casey's small, heart-shaped face grew anxious. "We can't stop now!" she pleaded. "We won't make the deadline!"

"Yeah," Hector said. "When are we going to finish the story?"

"Tomorrow morning," Tina said, "before my party. We'll make the deadline. I promise."

That night, Casey lay in bed, staring into the blackness above her. She kept thinking about the Slime Monster story. It was a great story, but what if they didn't get it done on time? What if they didn't win? She tried to push the thoughts out of her mind.

Casey turned onto her left side and punched her pillow so it would fluff up under her cheek. There. Nice and comfy. Just perfect for sleeping. But then she started to worry about her missing Slime Monster doll. If one of her friends hadn't taken it, where could it be? She wasn't sure she even wanted to know the answer to that question.

Casey was getting mad at herself now. At this rate, she was never going to get any sleep. She rolled over onto her right side and stared at the strange shapes her toys made in the dark. Her train set, lying on its side, looked like a wiggly snake. Her baseball mitt, sitting on top of her desk, resembled a giant clam. Even stranger, her teddy bear, standing in the middle of the carpet, seemed to be moving toward her!

Casey sucked in her breath and lay still. Her eyes were playing tricks on her, she told herself. Her mother said she had an overactive imagination.

"You laughing at me?" a harsh voice whispered. "You laughing at *me*?"

Casey's heart jumped. That wasn't her teddy bear. It was Gooey Gus, and he was alive! Casey leaped at the lamp on the night table and fumbled to turn it on.

Though the light was dim, it still took a moment for Casey's eyes to adjust. She focused again on the spot where she'd seen the Slime Monster, but there was nothing there. And her teddy bear was sitting in the far corner of the room on top of the toy chest.

Casey's heart was trying to pound its way out of her chest, the same way Gooey Gus had broken down the door of Gaby's room! But wait a minute. That wasn't real. That was in the story they were writing. Casey was starting to get confused.

Casey turned the light out and lay back down. She was probably also confused about what she'd seen in the dark. And heard.

"Overactive imagination," Casey told herself, rolling over onto her stomach and pushing the pillow away. "That's definitely what it was." Casey closed her eyes and stared at the insides of her eyelids.

It was a long, long time before she finally fell asleep.

Okay!" Tina said early the next morning as she bounced into Jamal's room. "So the team's trying to escape from the bodega, and the Slime Monster just kicked the door open."

"Right," Alex said as Tina took her place in front of Jamal's computer. "Any second now, the Slime Monster's gonna spew, and it's curtains."

Casey, who was lying on Jamal's bed, yawned.

"What's the matter?" asked Lenni, who was sitting at the foot of the bed. "Don't you think this is exciting? I do." Lenni had finished reading the new additions to the story.

Casey's eyes looked big and glazed. "Uh, sure," she said.

Jamal looked at his cousin with concern. "You've got puffy circles under your eyes. You feel okay?"

Casey didn't answer. She was beginning to be sorry she'd ever started this Slime Monster story in the first place. It had been fun when it was just a Gotcha game, but if it got any scarier, she might never sleep again.

"Come on," Hector said to Tina. "It's time to knock out the Slime Monster for good."

"Yeah," Gaby said. "What's his weakness?"

"Well, cold stuff," Casey said, worried. "But he's six feet tall, he's big and strong, and he's burning mad . . ." *In the story,* she told herself.

"What if he *weren't* angry," Lenni mused.

"What do you mean?" Alex asked.

Lenni twisted a strand of hair around and around her finger. "Well," she began thoughtfully, "he's this creepy-looking monster who's afraid everyone's laughing at him. If suddenly everyone were *nice* to him . . ."

Tina's eyes lit up. "Maybe he wouldn't be angry! I'll try it!"

Tina twisted around in her chair to face the keyboard. She began to write:

The team cowered in fear as the Slime Monster burst into the bodega. He seemed to have grown even taller in the heat outside. His head grazed the ceiling, leaving a trail of purple goo. His humongous hands knocked cans and boxes off the shelves of the bodega.

"You laughing at me?" he boomed in his powerful voice. "You laughing at *me*?"

Tina bravely stepped forward. "Uh, excuse me, Mr. Slime Monster, sir," she said.

Gooey Gus's eyes crawled through the slime on his face in order to focus on Tina. "What do *you* want?" he demanded.

"I just wanted to point out that no one's laughing."

If the monster had had eyebrows, they would have shot up in surprise. He cupped his hand to his ear stubs and craned his neck, listening. "I'm sure somebody's laughing, somewhere," he insisted.

Jamal stepped forward, joining Tina. "Why would they laugh?" he asked in that logical voice of his.

"Just look at me!" the Slime Monster said. "I'm all twisted and gooey and purple. I'm hideous!"

Stepping carefully to avoid the goo, Gaby also came forward. "*I* don't think so," she said. She was lying, of course, but, hey, when your life is at stake, you do what you gotta do! And, anyway, the Slime Monster seemed to be feeling a little better.

"You really don't think I'm hideous?" he asked.

"Really," Gaby assured him. "Purple is my favorite color!"

The Slime Monster sighed and leaned heavily upon the counter. He was dripping slime all over the cash register and the open box of breath mints, but no one had the nerve to tell him. Then a shiny purple tear dropped out of one bloodshot eye.

"It's not that easy being purple," he said sadly. "People call me all kinds of nasty names. Mr. Eggplant. Grape Boy." Tears were coming faster now, lumping and bumping down the ridges of his face. "And worst of all, they always confuse me with that doofy dinosaur!"

The Slime Monster hid his face in his hands and began to blubber loudly. The kids surrounded him and gingerly patted his black rubber raincoat, careful not to let any slime touch their skin.

"It's okay, Slimy," Alex comforted him.

"Yeah," Hector said. "We're your friends."

"Gimme a break!" Alex said as he read the screen over Tina's shoulder. "This is supposed to be a horror story. We can't end it with everybody crying and hugging each other."

Jamal made a kissy face. "I love you, Slimy!" he said, smooching the air.

Even Casey, lying exhausted on the bed, found

the energy to complain. "Where's the atmosphere? Where's the suspense?"

"We need a *big* ending," Hector declared. "Like an explosion or something."

Tina nodded. She blocked out most of what she'd just written and pressed the Delete button. "So, let's try something else," she said. "Any suggestions?"

"What's the Slime Monster afraid of?" Gaby asked. "Maybe we could scare him with something."

"Worms?" Jamal suggested.

"Snakes!" cried Lenni.

Alex started writing down the suggestions in his casebook.

Hector's eyes grew wide. "How 'bout an even *bigger* Slime Monster? But one who's fighting for the team."

Ghostwriter flew onto Alex's notebook and rearranged some letters.

Melt him.

Alex read Ghostwriter's idea aloud.

Casey, clutching Jamal's pillow like a teddy bear, sat up on the bed. "I like that. Let's melt him down until he's a drippy, slimy glob. That'll fix him."

"Not necessarily," Jamal pointed out. "He likes heat, remember? It makes him stronger."

Tina smiled. "What if we put ice directly on *him*, like we did with the gum?"

"That makes sense," Gaby agreed.

"I'm gonna try it," Tina said as she began to type.

The team cowered in fear as the Slime Monster burst into the bodega. He seemed to have grown even taller in the heat outside. His head grazed the ceiling, leaving a trail of purple goo. His humongous hands knocked cans and boxes off the shelves of the bodega.

"You laughing at me?" he boomed in his powerful voice. "You laughing at *me*?"

"Quick, everybody!" Tina shouted. "To the freezer!"

The kids raced to the freezer and opened all the glass doors. They started yanking out bags of ice and frozen vegetables, boxes of ice cream, and TV dinners. As fast as they could get them out, they threw them at the Slime Monster.

The Slime Monster started to shiver. He pulled his raincoat more tightly around himself. "Brrrrrrrr!" he said. "So cold! So cold!"

"It's working!" Hector shouted.

Encouraged, the team kept pelting the monster with frozen things. He started to back away.

"That's right, Slimy!" Alex yelled as Gooey Gus retreated out the back door. "Get lost!"

The Slime Monster staggered down the sidewalk. Alex and the others closed the door and locked it, though it still had a huge, gaping hole in the middle from where Gus had punched through it.

Jamal watched through the hole as the Slime

Monster disappeared around the corner. "I wonder where he's going," he said.

"Yeah," Tina agreed. "Now that he's outside
where it's warm, he'll get his strength back. We
have to stop him before he attacks his next victim."

"I pity that person," Jamal said, "whoever it is."

Upstairs in the loft, Lenni was on the cordless
phone with her dad.

"I'm sorry, honey," Max Frazier was saying to
her, "but my rehearsal's going to go a little later
than I thought. I don't think I'll make it home till ten
o'clock. You gonna be okay all alone there by
yourself?"

Lenni laughed. Her father was so over-
protective. She already baby-sat for some of the
little kids in the neighborhood. She could certainly
take care of herself.

"I'll be fine, Dad," she assured him. "Don't worry
about a thing."

Downstairs at the bodega, Jamal was getting
ready to leave. "I'm gonna head home and take
another look at that chunk of frozen slime," he told
the others. "Maybe it will help me figure out a way
to stop Gooey Gus."

"Meanwhile," Hector said, "the rest of us should
follow the Slime Monster."

Alex looked worried. "I don't know if that's a

good idea. He nearly slimed us before. What if he tries again?"

Lenni, who'd hung up the phone with her father, was now sitting at her electric piano, doodling on the keyboard. While she played, she sang the new song she and Tuan were going to perform at Tina's party:

"A feeling like this, you know, it's never going to end,
'Cause nothing's going to stop the love of friends."

She was so wrapped up in her music, she didn't notice what was creeping under the front door. Purple slime oozed slowly but purposefully across the wooden floor.

Lenni sang on. "Nothing's gonna stop, nothing's gonna stop . . ."

Nothing was going to stop the slime as it got closer and closer and closer, reaching hungrily for Lenni's juicy feet. Then the door burst open.

Lenni turned around, and when she saw who'd come to visit, she screamed.

"Aaaaaaaaaaaaaaaah!"

Chapter Twelve

"Aaaaaaaaaaaaaaaah!"

Downstairs in the bodega, the Ghostwriter Team heard Lenni's scream.

"He's upstairs!" Gaby exclaimed. "The Slime Monster's got Lenni!"

"We have to save her!" Casey declared. They ran outside and up the staircase that led to the front door of Lenni's loft.

The long wooden desk in Jamal's room was completely buried under test tubes, beakers, a microscope, and all kinds of stuff he'd borrowed from the kitchen. Inside a cooler filled with ice were clear plastic bags containing chunks of frozen slime. There was a cheese grater, a garlic press, a rolling pin, lemon juice, paint thinner, vinegar, and a pair of tweezers. It looked as if Jamal was either cooking dinner or planning to blow up the world.

Jamal, wearing a football helmet and swim goggles, carefully sliced a piece of frozen slime with a penknife. He placed the slice in a clear glass dish, then poured vinegar over it. He swished the vinegar around, waiting to see if it would dissolve the slime, but nothing happened.

Jamal crossed vinegar off the long list of things he'd tried. Nothing had worked so far. Was the Slime Monster completely invulnerable? Impossible! But trial and error wasn't working. Maybe it was time to do some research. Fortunately, Jamal had a complete set of encyclopedias in his bedroom. Without getting off his desk chair, he rolled over to his bookshelf and took out the *G* volume.

Quickly flipping to *Gum,* Jamal scanned the article. If he could find something on how to destroy gum, they'd have a chance of destroying the Slime Monster.

Before he had read very far, Ghostwriter's bright light streaked into the room and rearranged the words on the page.

HELP! LENNI'S IN TROUBLE!

Jamal knew what that meant. The Slime Monster had gotten her, and time was running out. Jamal searched through the mess on his desk for a pen. He couldn't find one, but he did find an old lipstick of his mother's that he'd been using for his experiment. Jamal quickly wrote with the lipstick on the back of a notebook:

"GW, HELP ME READ!"

Ghostwriter changed the letters back on the page of the encyclopedia, then his green glow traveled over the words while Jamal read:

Gum: Standard chewing gum consists of five basic ingredients: gum base, sugar, corn syrup, softeners, and flavorings. Gum base does not dissolve during chewing. It makes gum chewy and acts as a base for other ingredients. Softeners, such as vegetable oil, keep the gum soft. Flavorings make the gum tasty.

Ghostwriter pulsed on the word *softeners,* but Jamal had already seen it.

"Exactly what I was thinking," Jamal said. He read further until he came to the part about vegetable oil. An idea was starting to form in his mind. Vegetable oil made the gum softer. Maybe he could use vegetable oil to *soften* the Slime Monster. If the Slime Monster got soft enough, he might fall apart! Of course, there was a chance this idea wouldn't work, but at this point, it was their only hope.

Jamal snapped the encyclopedia shut. "Let's

go, Ghostwriter!" he said, knowing his friend would sense that he was leaving. Tucking the encyclopedia under his arm, Jamal ran out the door with Ghostwriter close behind.

When the team got to the top of the stairs, the first thing they noticed was that the front door to the loft was wide open. This was a bad sign. A very bad sign. Tina, the first through the door, motioned the others to be quiet as they entered.

The sea of purple slime all over the floor told them everything they needed to know. The Slime Monster had been there. But there was no sign of him or Lenni now.

Stepping carefully around the slime, and fearing the worst, the team searched for their friend.

"Hlllp," came a muffled moan.

Everyone heard it, but no one could tell where it was coming from. Was it possible, really possible, that Lenni might still be alive?

"Hlllp!"

It was louder now, and definitely recognizable as Lenni's voice. But why couldn't they find her?

Casey, who was nearest the wide-open front door, pushed it closed. That's when they saw what had happened to Lenni. Hanging off the back of the door was a bumpy purple cocoon, roughly the size of a twelve-year-old girl. It was hard to tell which bumps were elbows or knees or feet.

The team rushed to the door, and Hector started to reach for Lenni.

"Don't touch her!" Gaby warned. "I know you want to help her, but we can't let the slime get on us."

"We can't leave her there!" Alex argued.

"Thslmmmstrsstlhr," Lenni said. The words weren't clear, but her fear was.

"What?" Hector asked.

Lenni spoke more clearly, trying to enunciate through the slime that covered her mouth. "Hs . . . stl . . . hr!"

Casey made a face. "Hisstilhir?"

Gaby suddenly realized what Lenni was trying to say. She turned fearfully to the Lenni-cocoon. "Did you say, *'He's still here?'*"

The purple mask of a face nodded slightly.

Everybody was thinking the same thing: *I'm next.* Maybe there was still time to run, but that wouldn't solve anything.

Casey was the first to speak. "Let's make sure he doesn't get out," she said bravely. "So he can't hurt anybody else."

Alex nodded. "It's us against him. The final battle."

"We have to get ready," Hector said, heading for the refrigerator in the kitchen area.

Gaby, Casey, and Alex were right behind them. They opened the door to the freezer and started pulling out ice cube trays, a bag of mixed vegetables, and a box of frozen pizza.

"Of course, this will only slow him down—" Gaby started to say.

Nobody heard the oven door slowly opening. Nobody saw the slimy purple mouth twisting and puckering as it got ready to spit.

SPLAT!

It happened so fast, nobody saw what hit them.

Chapter Thirteen

Jamal wasn't able to get in the front door of the bodega because it was still blockaded. He entered through the hole in the back door. Treading quietly through the storeroom, he gently pushed open the swinging doors and peered into the empty store.

It looked like the aftermath of a nuclear war. The floor was covered with melting frozen food and slimy footprints. The doors to the freezers were gaping open, and there were bags of rice and cardboard boxes blocking the front door. The phone receiver, with its burnt, severed cord, lay on the wooden counter near a slimed-over box of breath mints.

Jamal listened carefully. Though it seemed as if no one was there, he knew what a slimy operator Gooey Gus was. Gus could be hiding, ready to pop out and surprise him with a mouthful of purple poison. There was no sound at all inside the bodega. No raspy breathing, no squishy footsteps, not even the muffled sound of cars honking outside on the street.

Jamal had to risk going in. There was something he needed, and he couldn't afford to wait. There were only a few spots on the floor that weren't covered with slime or melting ice. Jumping from one to another, Jamal made his way to the shelf with the vegetable oil.

There were half a dozen bottles filled with the clear yellow fluid. Jamal tried to stuff them all into his knapsack, but only four would fit. Slinging the heavy canvas sack over his shoulder, he held the other two bottles in his hands. It was a lot harder to avoid the slime carrying all the oil, but Jamal managed to make it to the back door without hurting himself or the bottles.

Thump! Thump! Thump!

The sounds were coming from upstairs in the loft. That must be where Lenni was! Jamal wondered if anyone else from the team was with her.

Jamal ran up the stairs to Lenni's loft. The front door was wide open. When Jamal walked through it, he gasped in horror. It wasn't the slime puddles all over the floor. It wasn't the frozen pizza melting beside the refrigerator. It was the big *thing* in the middle of the room. The big, purple, slimy, lumpy thing with four heads and four faces, shuffling and bumping and moaning. It didn't take Jamal long to figure out that it was all that was left of the Ghostwriter Team. Gooey Gus had slimed them all into one big glob.

Then Jamal noticed the smaller slimy blob hanging off the back of the front door. He couldn't tell which of his friends it was, but he guessed it was Lenni. She must have been attacked first, then the others got it while they were trying to save her.

So Jamal and Ghostwriter were the only ones left. Ghostwriter flew out of the *G* encyclopedia Jamal still carried and circled the big group blob. His aura turned from green to red and pulsed in distress. He could sense the terrible fear of his slowly suffocating friends.

Jamal's first instinct was to try to free them, but he knew it would be of no use unless he got rid of Gooey Gus first. And Jamal knew the monster was still in the apartment. Gus wouldn't leave with the job unfinished. Gus was waiting for him.

Jamal was ready. Uncapping the two bottles of vegetable oil in his hands, Jamal tiptoed around the slime puddles on the floor, searching for the monster.

"Psssst!"

Jamal whirled around, bracing for attack, but no one was there. So, Gooey Gus was playing games. Jamal continued his search, all his senses alert.

"Psssst! Jamal! Over here!"

The whispered voice was coming from the direction of the laundry room. A pair of brown eyes and a long, straight lock of shiny black hair were just visible around the door frame.

"Tina!" Jamal exclaimed joyfully. At least one of his friends was still unharmed.

"Shhh!" Tina warned, motioning him to come closer.

Jamal tiptoed over to her. "How'd you . . . ?"

"I hid before he saw me," she answered. "But the rest of the team . . . it was horrible!" Tears glistened in Tina's eyes as she remembered.

Jamal, too, felt a lump rise in his throat at the thought of his friends suffering, and slowly dying. "Is he still here?" Jamal asked.

Tina nodded. "I'm just not sure where."

Jamal handed Tina a bottle of vegetable oil. "Here."

Tina studied it, confused. "What are we gonna do, make a salad?"

"No," Jamal whispered. "This stuff will soften up Gus enough for us to send him back where he came from."

Tina didn't look convinced. In truth, Jamal wasn't either, but it was the only chance they had. "Trust me," Jamal said, hoping he sounded convincing. "I'm a scientist. And I've got a plan."

"What?" Tina asked.

Jamal began to whisper in her ear. He couldn't afford to let the Slime Monster overhear what he was telling her.

Seconds later, Tina was nowhere in sight. Jamal, holding up a plastic laundry basket in front of him like a shield, cautiously made his way around the apartment. "C'mon, Grape Boy," he called bravely, trying to goad the monster out of hiding. "Come on out! I'm gonna chew you up and spit you out, Gus!"

The only answer was an eerie silence. Gus was playing possum.

Jamal crept toward the kitchen. "I'm not afraid of you!" he lied. "In fact, I'm *laughing* at you. Ha ha ha! Come on, Slimy. Ha ha ha ha ha ha!"

Still, Gus didn't answer. *What is he waiting for?* Jamal wondered. *Is the Slime Monster pretending he's not here just to get me off guard?*

Suddenly the cabinet doors beneath the sink flew open, and the Slime Monster burst out and tried to grab Jamal. Jamal was just able to slip out of the clutching purple fingers and run to the other side of the island in the middle of the kitchen. Gooey Gus lurched after him.

"You laughing at me?" he thundered. "You laughing at *me*?"

Jamal was terrified, but he used his karate wisdom to keep cool. If he couldn't think clearly, he couldn't enact his plan. Jamal slowly backed away from the monster, keeping close to the island.

"Yeah," Jamal said, trying to sound brave. "I'm laughing, bubblehead. Ha ha ha!"

The Slime Monster stomped closer. "I'm *burning* mad!" he announced. "I'm *steaming* mad!"

Jamal backed up a few more steps.

"Slime, anyone?" the monster asked.

"Now!" Jamal shouted.

Tina leaped up onto the counter from the other side of the island and dumped a whole bottle of vegetable oil on top of the Slime Monster's head. The flowing oil began to leave a gradually deepening indentation in the middle of his head.

"Owwwwwwwww!" Gooey Gus wailed, raising his hands to shield his head. The oil began to eat through his fingers, too. Jamal and Tina stared with a mixture of horror and disgust.

Tina quickly grabbed a second bottle and continued to pour the oil on Gus. The top of his head was now almost completely gone, and his hands had been reduced to stumps. Gus sank to the floor and hid what was left of his head beneath his arms. Sensing his opportunity, Jamal put his knapsack on the counter and pulled out a third bottle of oil, which he dumped on Gus.

"You laughing at me?" Gus moaned as his arms and head melted together into a gooey lump. His back and legs started to dissolve, too. "You laughing at me! . . ." came his final plaintive wail as the last of him melted away into a purple puddle.

The puddle bubbled briefly, then went flat and

still. Jamal and Tina stood over it, not quite sure the monster was dead. Tentatively, Jamal dipped the toe of his sneaker into the puddle, ready to kick it off if the slime started to creep up. But the slime was no more alive than a chewed-up piece of grape bubble gum.

"We did it!" Tina exclaimed, throwing her arms around Jamal. He hugged her back, hard. The nightmare was really, finally, over.

Tina and Jamal freed the others. And after they'd mopped up the mess and each had had a long shower, they were as good as new. But none of them would ever forget the horror that was Gooey Gus, the Slime Monster!

THE END

Chapter Fourteen

As Tina typed the final words of the story, the team applauded. Ghostwriter glowed purple on the computer screen where he, too, had been reading along.

"Great ending, Tina," Hector congratulated her.

Casey nodded soberly. "All of us slimed together . . . This story's gotten a lot scarier since the 'Gotcha' game I wrote at the beginning. And we finished by the deadline! I'll mail it in tomorrow morning."

Tina felt proud, but she shrugged modestly. "Glad I could help." She stood up and stretched. "Well, I'd better go get ready for my party. Don't be late, you guys."

"Are you kidding?" Alex said. "I didn't eat breakfast this morning 'cause I knew how good the food's gonna be tonight. Are you making those little barbecued spareribs like you did last summer? Or what about those fried shrimp balls in that special sauce?"

Gaby rolled her eyes. "Alex is a human encyclopedia of every food he ever ate."

"Me too," Jamal chimed in. "What's cookin'?"

"You'll see," Tina said mysteriously. "I'll see you guys soon."

An hour later, Tina, Alex, Gaby, Lenni, Jamal, Casey, Hector, and Tina's brother, Tuan, were gathered on the roof of Tina's building. Lenni was playing on her synthesizer keyboard while Tuan accompanied her on his electric guitar. Gaby was teaching Tina some dance moves she'd just made up. Ghostwriter, hovering in the air above the team, bopped in time to the funky beat. Tuan, of course, couldn't see Ghostwriter dancing. Nobody could except the Ghostwriter Team.

A few yards away, Casey and Hector were kicking a soccer ball back and forth. Jamal and Alex stood next to the food, inhaling spring rolls.

"These *cha-gio* are fantastic!" Alex said as he sunk his teeth into the crispy, fried dough.

Jamal nodded as he gobbled a shrimp ball. "Tina and her mother are great cooks!"

Alex glanced hungrily over at the barbecue grill. The rounded, black metal lid was closed, but steam escaped around the edges. Alex sniffed the air.

"Mmm," he said. "I wonder how many more minutes till the spareribs are ready."

Tina, overhearing Alex, smiled. "Okay, okay," she said, breaking away from Gaby and heading for the grill. "I'll see if they're done."

Casey licked her lips and followed close behind Tina. Alex and Jamal moved closer to the grill.

"I can almost taste them," Alex said as Tina put on an oven mitt and started to lift the lid.

Gaby joined them by the grill and sniffed the air. "What's that funny—"

As Tina pushed the lid all the way up, the kids' mouths dropped open in horror. There was something sizzling on the blackened metal slats of the grill, but it wasn't spareribs. It was the bumpy, twisted, purple face of Gooey Gus, the Slime Monster! He grinned hideously at the kids with his three snaggly teeth.

"Slime, anyone?" he asked as he rose up out of the grill.

The kids screamed and ran toward the stairs as the Slime Monster unleashed a tidal wave of purple goo.

Ghostwriter, floating above the barbecue, felt a powerful surge of fear wash over him. His friends were in trouble! But something more disturbing kept him from following them. In the blackness below him, he was starting to see—actually *see* something. It wasn't a word or a sentence or some free-floating letters. It was a color—purple—and a shape. Ghostwriter flew closer, straining to see. Since he'd awakened as a ghost, he'd never seen anything but words.

But now he could make out a face! A face with bulging, reddened eyes and horribly distorted features. Ghostwriter screamed in horror.

Gooey Gus heard the scream and stared back at the free-floating green glowing light. The light was shuddering and shivering, but not half as much as Gus when he realized what he was looking at. Gooey Gus, too, opened his mouth to scream.

"Aaaaaaaah! A ghost!"

Amazing Toy Company
466 Lexington Avenue
New York, NY

Dear Slime Monster People,

Here is our story for the Slime Monster contest.
My friends and I worked on it together, and
we think it's so scary, your hair will stand on
end! We put in atmosphere, suspense, obstacles,
and even a trick ending. We wrote it so it was
a story-in-a-story: the Ghostwriter Team writes
a story about themselves and the Slime Monster. Were you fooled when we made it look
like we'd finished writing the story and went to
Tina's party? That whole party scene where the
Slime Monster sees Ghostwriter was part of the
story, too! Gotcha!

Oh, and by the way, in case you were wonder-
ing: We made up Ghostwriter. He's not real or
anything. But of course you knew that. There's
no such thing as ghosts any more than there's
a real live Slime Monster!

I hope we win.

Yours truly,

Casey Austin

Hey, kids!
Don't miss the next exciting Ghostwriter adventure . . .

The Man Who Vanished

by Amy Keyishian

A horror author may have come to a horrifying end!

Alex and Tina are thrilled to get the chance to meet writer Emory Rex. Then Rex vanishes from the middle of a packed horror convention. The rest of the Ghostwriter Team must help their friends find the missing writer. Using clues from the author's own books, the team starts closing in on Rex—and running into some frighteningly weird suspects. If the team doesn't find the writer, they'll never know how his latest scary story ends. . . .